The Stone Murders

THE
STONE
MURDERS

MATTI JOENSUU

*Translated from Finnish by
Raili Taylor*

A
Joan
Kahn
BOOK

**St. Martin's Press
New York**

COPYEDITED BY: Jane K. Mollman

Design by Jessica Winer

Library of Congress Cataloging-in-Publication Data

Joensuu, Matti Yrjänä, 1948–
    The stone murders.
    "A Joan Kahn Book"
    Translation of: Harjunpää ja poliisin poika.
I. Title.
PH355.J553H2813   1987   894'.54133   87-4471
ISBN 0-312-00689-6

    First published in Finland in 1983 by Otava under the title *Harjunpää ja poliisin poika*. English translation first published in Great Britain in 1986 by Victor Gollancz Ltd. under the title *Harjunpaa and the Stone Murders*.

First U.S. Edition

10 9 8 7 6 5 4 3 2 1

The Stone Murders

1

"I said to him, 'No, we're animals.'" Leo spoke so unex-
pectedly and so loudly that Mikael was startled. "Wasn't
that great!"

Mikael furtively increased his pace, aware of Leo's
tone. It demanded a response, even a look. But he neither answered nor looked at Leo. There was something
else on his mind: All night long he had hoped they would
talk about what had happened, he had almost prayed
they would, and now, when Leo finally seemed to be hint-
ing at it, he no longer wished to hear—he didn't even
want to think about it. He'd rather it didn't exist, that
nothing had happened.

"We're animals!"

Now Leo sounded angry. And he had stopped, you
could tell without looking. Mikael chewed his lip; the way
the man's voice rang in his ears, he wanted them to
hurry, to get away, anywhere, even home.

"Do you hear me, Miku?"

"Yes, yes. Don't bloody shout so."

"Why shouldn't I? All you shits in Kontula, sleep well!"

The shout ricocheted like a bullet from the nearest
house. Mikael had to stop. His hands were clenched so
tight he could feel the pulse beating in the palm of his
hand. He wanted, fervently, to avoid the whole issue.
Now he didn't even feel drunk any more, he was only
pretending to be drunk. As a matter of fact he knew he
had been sober for hours, he had only been playacting,

1

all the time, ever since he got on the bus in the city center. He turned to say something to Leo but couldn't meet his eye.

Instead he stared past Leo, toward the shopping center, and suddenly he knew perfectly well why they had been hanging around there for hours: They had wanted everyone to notice them and remember them and to say that they had been there all the time. And not just since the last bus.

Mikael breathed in so hard his cheeks trembled.

He wished that it was morning, that he had had a good night's sleep, and when he woke his father would be in a good mood and say, "As it's Saturday why don't we drive into town and buy you those drums you're always going on about. . . ." But it wasn't morning yet—only a weak light in the east. And when Mikael shifted his gaze he saw Leo.

Leo was sixteen already, two years older than Mikael. He was skinny and very tall, even though he always hunched his shoulders and didn't stand straight. He seemed pliable, like those rubber skeletons you find in joke shops. He wore trainers and jeans but no shirt. Instead Leo had a waistcoat that he boasted having pinched from somebody's balcony. And he had a black peaked cap, like a chauffeur. You couldn't see Leo's eyes beneath the peak but you always felt he could see yours. Leo's face was also long and pimply. He wanted to be called Sid but Mikael never remembered.

With the way Leo looked most people preferred to step aside when they saw him coming.

"You know something?" Leo spoke sharply and Mikael got an uneasy feeling they were no longer mates. He swallowed with difficulty and when Leo noticed it his eyes narrowed.

"You know you're called Miku because it suits you better than Mikael." Leo was chuckling. "You're no angel, you're even better than your brother, a right little devil!"

Leo's cackle was fast and rasping. Then he moved on, pulling Mikael with him, a hand on his shoulder. At the touch Mikael felt immediately better. They were together again, mates, even their steps sounded as one. He was tempted to skip a little.

"I was so drunk," he laughed. "Never been so drunk in my life. My head is still spinning. . . ."

"We were fast, no hanging about. We had some action."

"Yeah. But we're not . . . not to anybody."

"You were real ace. But I wasn't too bad neither. I said to him 'We're animals.' You think that berk really thought . . ."

Leo's voice trailed off and Mikael looked up. In Leo's grinning face his eyes were mere slits, he shook with laughter. Mikael wanted to join in. He wanted to laugh as they had earlier, at the shopping center, like Leo now, laugh and laugh until there was no breath left and still laugh even when it hurt. But he couldn't even get started. Nothing happened, however hard he tried. And only a few hours earlier it had been enough if one or the other had said: "Excuse me, sir, can we use your bottle-opener?" That had been enough to set them off.

"Do you think he really took us for animals?" Leo asked through his laughter. "Like we was bears! Or tigers . . . Sugar Frosties tigers from a packet of Kellogg's. Look out, the Sugar Frosties tiger's coming, it's jumping on the table. Listen you kids, get those Frosties down your gob!"

Mikael was shaken, staring at Leo. His heart beat so fast it was painful. It had felt like this last April when he had been caught shoplifting and he had had to wait for two hours in the shop for his father to come and take him home. Now he had the same feeling in his belly, it was

3

like a tight bag, fit to burst. He could not help thinking that maybe this was the way the man had felt after going down. Mikael swayed uncertainly for a moment and then sprinted off, fast and speechless, but he hadn't gone ten yards before Leo caught up with him.

"Not that way." Leo was still laughing. "Don't be afraid of the Sugar Frosties tiger, no need. Let's go to my place, there might be something left over from my mum. I'd like something, I'd like to get really drunk. Come on."

"No, I must get home. My old man."

"Shit, Jani was never afraid of him. He used to say that one day he'll smash his head in with his own truncheon. Come on."

"No. I must."

Mikael pulled himself free. He didn't dare to look at Leo again, but moved away with difficulty, as if something was holding him back. He could hear Leo's mocking imitation, "I must."

"Clear off then!" Leo said. "That's what your brother did, too."

This was said with such vehemence that Mikael couldn't understand what Leo meant.

Mikael had got only far enough to see the pond and the wooden frogs around it when the sound made him stop. Te-te-te! Fast and electric. The sound was not loud and yet it pierced his ear like a needle. It came from his pocket. He had forgotten all about it.

Mikael looked around, worried that someone else had heard it. But he was alone. The footpath was empty and dark; farther back was the gable end of the house where Leo lived. Mikael thought hard, only now he realized that he'd need to explain that sound—and that his father would not believe any explanations.

Mikael's mouth felt dry. With rigid fingers he undid the breast pocket of his jeans jacket and pulled out a watch. His lips formed the words: "Zero three, zero one and twenty-five. Alarm Melody Chro-no-graph."

He tilted his head.

It was a good watch, its dial shaped like a TV screen, the same gray color, and the black numbers seemed to appear from nowhere. It had a metal wristband and made a nice clinking sound. It was just the sort of watch he had wanted, knowing that he would never get one— Sod never bought him anything, he hoarded all his money, apart from what he drank; he owned at least three flats, which he let.

"Zero three, zero one and fifty."

Mikael's grip tightened on the watch and he shut his eyes.

Actually he didn't want the watch, it had no game function, it was nothing special. It didn't even feel nice, it was almost slimy, and after a while the changing numbers looked as exciting as the blinking eye of a lizard. He should have let Leo keep the watch and see if there was something better in the pockets.

Mikael opened first his eyes and then his fist.

The watch fell down and shone between his shoes like some fallen star. Suddenly Mikael was full of hatred for the watch, furiously full, so full he wanted to grind his heel over it and hear the glass break and see the blinking numbers stop forever. He gasped and lifted his heel to ram it down—but there was something on his trouser leg, something he hadn't noticed before. Mikael looked closer, lifting his leg up.

The bottoms of his trouser legs were splattered with spots. Small spots, now almost black; only the rims remained red. It could have been paint.

Mikael felt the shock in his belly. It made his knees buckle. He couldn't move, he could hardly breathe. Sweat was pouring from his forehead.

5

He sat down, spat on his fingers, and busily rubbed the fabric with his spit. Gravel on the path crunched under him; the sound of rubbing was as loud as his breathing.

But the spots would not go away.

Some of them spread and joined together, forming a brownish red mess.

Mikael was stunned, he couldn't even stand. His eyes were wide, his mouth half open. When breathing finally came more easily he muttered, in a half-suppressed cry, "Shit, he wouldn't have got any drums anyway."

2

"Sorry."

Harjunpaa had said sorry umpteen times and now shifted uneasily. The man did not try again. Instead he laid his arm on the table and gestured to Harjunpaa. His gesture seemed to mean you try for yourself.

His arm was tanned. It was a strong arm, used to lifting and carrying, its muscles well developed. It was an arm used to hard work, and although it now rested on the table, it glistened with sweat, as if under stress. Veins were pulsating close to the surface; they seemed to be transmitting some coded message. Harjunpaa moved unobtrusively back in his chair. He did not want to touch the arm. The mere thought repelled him, and besides, he knew it would be dishonest. He was by now quite certain that the man wasn't sane.

"You try, feel the veins. You can feel how the stuff is multiplying."

Harjunpaa pressed his fingertips to his forehead. Since the last call he had had an hour in the rest room, without sleep. That had been the third cot death he had come across, a boy, six weeks old. They hadn't called the police surgeon, instead they had taken the baby straight in to wait for an autopsy. Harko had driven the patrol car, Harjunpaa sitting next to him, holding the little bundle, wrapped in towels, in his lap. Yet he did not feel sleepy now, only tired. He wished he could get up without another word, walk out and sit somewhere, blanking his mind out while watching the sunrise over the sleeping city. That was out of the question. He had to speak, to say: "This has nothing to do with the police. We can't help you, you need a doctor, a psychiatrist." And he had no way of saying this without causing pain.

Harjunpaa managed to muster his thoughts but before he had time to speak he was distracted by the beeper in his pocket; it squealed like a small animal in pain. He stood up, sending the chair clattering behind him with an irritating noise. He was not yet used to this form of remote control; the squeal gave him a shock every time, had him believe something really awful had happened. He put out his hand to the phone but changed his mind. Instead he walked around the table and went to the door. "Sorry," he said yet again, as he left the room. At first he walked quickly down the corridor, then slowed down. He felt he had made a temporary escape and wanted to prolong this break between two unpleasant situations.

As soon as he entered the control room Harjunpaa knew this was not one of those deaths common just before dawn. Harko had been summoned as well, and the duty officer would not have called them both in for an ordinary death. As Harjunpaa pulled the door open the duty officer put the telephone receiver down and continued to write a dispatch note.

"Fourteen," he said, without looking up.

"Still in the water," added Harko. "In Kaisaniemi Bay. Face gone black already, they say. Some fisherman reported it. A patrol car from Eira is there already."

Harko looked half-asleep and annoyed; one might have thought he had a grudge against all who moved on the waters early in the morning. He was shivering after his interrupted sleep and had to strike two matches before his cigarette would light.

"What's wrong with that guy in there?" he asked, "mad or something?"

"I guess you could put him under thirteen. . . . Better ask somebody from the technical department to come along, since we'll need to have his fingers cut off. I'll clear that man out."

Harjunpaa didn't go into the interview room again, he remained at the doorway, hoping that the man would understand. He had to clear his throat; somehow he felt guilty and uneasy.

"I do hope you won't misunderstand this but I have to say . . ." he began, and saw the change in the man's face as he stood up. For a moment there was scorn, then sadness, before it became a face of a man turned away a thousand times.

"You know as well as I do that there is no such vaccine," Harjunpaa continued, averting his eyes. "And you know there is no reason why just you would be given such a vaccine if it existed. And I believe you know also what's at the root of all this, all your troubles have caused stress . . . and possibly your drinking—"

The man pushed past Harjunpaa, out of the room. He covered his face with his hand, as if to protect it from something—a slap, a tear, words fighting to get through. With tiredness in his steps he made his way down the corridor, toward the reception area, now tinted red with the dawn. It seemed to Harjunpaa, walking behind him, that his head and shoulders were shaking. Harjunpaa wanted to say something more but there were no suitable words; too many years had passed and the words had been used so often all meaning had worn off. All the same he tried once they reached the lobby, "If you can't get any help from the doctors . . . why don't you come back some day next week, during the day. We could talk things over . . ."

The man didn't stop, didn't even turn his head, and the card Harjunpaa had given him fluttered down to the floor, a useless piece of litter.

9

The sun was already up. It splashed the building site across the road with orange light, and when the man reached the bottom of the steps and the street he, too, was tinted red.

Harjunpaa stood still for a while. The feeling of guilt, which a moment earlier had dried his throat, had now settled further down, turned into a hard little knot behind his diaphragm. He felt he had been an unwitting catalyst in some chain of events, otherwise quite unconnected with him—or that at least he had been unable to stop something from happening. He was sure he should have acted somehow, should have tried, although he had no idea what he could have done. Harjunpaa rubbed his forehead, sensing the huge police station around him—full of gray corridors leading you back where you had started from; doors where your knock was never answered, telephones ringing to no avail. A building full of scanners and hidden closed-circuit TV cameras that followed everything you did or didn't do. Harjunpaa felt lost, in a wrong place; suddenly he no longer even knew the way to the underground car park.

"Timo! They're waiting for you in the car park. They asked you to hurry." Harjunpaa turned. The duty officer had clambered over the counter and was standing by the big glass door. Harjunpaa cleared his throat; he felt he had been caught doing something forbidden. It was already ten past five and he quickened his pace down the corridor that took him to the elevators. He hurried simply because a body long soaked in the sea could easily keep them busy for several hours—and there were now barely three hours till eight o'clock and the end of his shift.

He also knew that now the night was almost over, the fire brigade would soon start reporting the deaths that had occurred in the night, discovered as people woke up.

The duty rooms were windowless and it felt wonderful to be in the open air: The whole world was full of

10

opaque, pinkish light, and when the car window was down you could tell it would be another hot, muggy day. It reminded you of what you had forgotten while inside: that it was summer, July, and the city was empty and quiet.

Thurman was driving. Harko sat next to him. Harjunpaa had the back all to himself. He rested his head against the window frame and felt his thoughts slipping away; soon he was only aware of the rattle of the car and the familiar streets whizzing by.

"And what was wrong with him?" Harko asked.

"Life, I suppose."

Harjunpaa would have preferred not to talk, but Harko turned round, leaning on his elbow, and looked back. His eyebrows were arched in a questioning way, and with a sigh Harjunpaa forced himself out of the oblivion he had nearly reached.

"He's a carpenter," he said quietly. "Unemployed for almost two years now. Last May he did some small jobs for a mate of his, for this mate's house; somebody told the social security that he'd got a steady job and there was some hassle about his bank account. He's got three children, all under seven. The wife is a cook but last month she slipped a disk and is now on sick leave, waiting to go into the hospital. There wasn't enough money so he sold his car and that money is now going down his throat. Always had a liking for a tipple."

They drove through the narrow streets. Pavements were littered with Friday night mementos: hot-dog wrappers, broken bottles, a pair of knickers. Newspapers were being delivered, a gray-haired man was pushing a cart loaded with boxes toward the market. Seagulls fought over something in the gutter but swallows were flying so high he could barely hear their joyful twittering.

"I think that drink was the real problem." Harjunpaa was almost talking to himself. "He's adamant that last

11

weekend an ambulance picked him up from the street and took him to some clinic where he was injected several times. These jabs contained something that multiplies inside him and eats him up, cell by cell. He believes he can feel it when he touches his veins."

"Sounds like he needs a shrink."

"I suppose so. But maybe it's worth a report all the same. What I think could have happened is that the police picked him up drunk and took him to the hangover clinic for a pick-me-up jab."

Thurman stopped on the bridge. By now the sun was yellow and its reflection on the sea glistened so brightly it didn't bear looking. To the right Kaisaniemi Bay was still. There was no wind.

"Now where exactly is that corpse supposed to be?" Thurman asked. Harko reached for the microphone.

"Patrol car from Eira, currently in Kaisaniemi. Can you hear car 8-9-1?"

"Yes, 127 can hear you."

The man who answered was young. He sounded breathless, as if he had just run to the car. But there was something else in his voice as well, something Harjunpaa could not analyze. He felt suddenly alert—not alarmed yet, but alert. For no apparent reason he found himself thinking that maybe they should have answered the call more quickly.

"What the hell's going on in there?" he muttered.

"Well, maybe it's the stink."

"Where exactly are you?" Harko spoke into the microphone. This time the answer came from another man, disgruntled, by the sound of it.

"By the waterside, where d'you think. Not far from the tracks. Close to Kaisaniemi Restaurant. Just come on down and do your job and we can all clear off."

"Will be down in a jiffy," replied Harko in a steady

12

voice. "Central, see that somebody's ready to receive the stiff."

Thurman started the car and took a sharp turn to the right. The trees on the roadside hid the sky; it was like driving into a green tunnel.

They could spot the patrol car far away. It was parked in a small sandy opening at the end of the road. One of the policemen was outside. The other sat at the wheel, leaning back, hands behind his head. With some relief Harjunpaa noted that there were no spectators yet. Thurman parked the car and Harjunpaa was first out.

"Morning, Harjunpaa from SUOPO."

"Lofman. We're from 1K."

Lofman was very young, barely in his twenties. After a sleepless night he looked like a scared kid. His uniform was still spotlessly blue and the lion badge in his cap shone in the sun.

"Look," Lofman muttered, avoiding Harjunpaa's eyes. "Somehow I think, maybe we should have made another report. . . ."

Harjunpaa stole a sideways glance at the police officer. The other policemen was in his fifties, gray with a pudgy face. His eyes were closed and you would have thought him asleep had he not been puffing a cigarette that was hanging from his mouth. Thurman walked up to the car and Harjunpaa heard him greet the other man: "Well, if it isn't Bergman!"

On one side of the opening ran a tarmac footpath. It followed the line of railway tracks all the way to the bottom of the bay. Beyond the footpath, along the waterline, were young lime trees and shrubs about six feet high. Harjunpaa edged his way through them, following Lofman. Dozens of sparrows were twittering among the bushes. Beyond the trees and parallel with them ran a sandy track.

13

"Of all the bloody shits one has to work with," Lofman said bitterly, as soon as they had reached the sand. He was almost in tears, maybe because he was so tired. "He cares for nothing, it's all the same to him. All he can think about is making it in time to the restaurant where he works as doorman, or getting to the bank before closing time to check that his rents have been paid, or how to maneuver an early retirement. And every bloody time I get something other than the usual beat, I'm lumbered with him. I'm bloody well going to quit Helsinki and . . ."

"Hey, take it easy, now." Harjunpaa didn't sound convincing. "It's no different anywhere else, you'll find one like him at every station. And if you wait a little, until you're his age, say ten years—"

By now he could smell the sea, thick and strong. The houses that lined the bay on the opposite side were surprisingly close. A small jetty stuck out over there, its end barely forty yards away. Gulls were bobbing on the water. Harjunpaa crossed the sandy path and came to a sloping shingle, about three yards wide. It wasn't very steep.

The corpse was down by the waterline. It had been a youngish man.

Harjunpaa stopped in his tracks; he knew instinctively that something was wrong.

He took a deep breath and could feel how tension rushed through his body and made his hair stand on end. A muscle in the corner of his eye twitched, once, twice, again and again; he rubbed it but to no avail—rubbing never helped.

The body lay on its side, almost in a fetal position. Only the feet were in water, up to the knees. His face was toward Harjunpaa, black as he had expected, but not in a way it should have been—it was black with dried blood.

"Oh damn."

"I knew there was something," Lofman said unhappily.

"But that shithead up there wouldn't even get out of the car to have a look."

"Harko," Harjunpaa shouted in a croaky voice. Harko rushed through the shrubbery, carrying an incident bag in his hand. He said nothing but his breathing was fast and noisy.

Harjunpaa looked around the shore. Some of the stones on the slope were small, some large; some were loose and showed a lighter side, as if they had recently been turned over. There were several of them around the body, particularly around his feet. Among the stones was broken glass—a beer bottle, judging by the color and label; a few steps away was a pink plastic carrier bag.

Harjunpaa looked up and down the strip of sand that formed the lower footpath. It looked the same in both directions—packed hard by thousands of indistinguishable footprints. But right where they were standing the sand was messed up, as though there had been a scuffle. Harjunpaa stepped back and Harko and Lofman followed him.

They could hear Thurman making his way through the thicket, jabbering as he came, "I said to Bergman that now he's paid for every minute he should remember the old times when . . . well, what's up?"

"He's not drowned." Once he had said it aloud Harjunpaa felt overcome by tiredness. "He's never been in the water, not the whole body, only his feet. He's been killed. And right here. Recently, too, last night."

"Bloody hell."

"There's no watch, only a white patch on his wrist."

"We'd better get some rope, and close off the footpath."

"I bet they tried to chuck him in the sea . . ."

"Norri must be told. And we must get the police surgeon here."

15

"I did write down the name and address of the fisherman who reported it."

"How was he killed?" Thurman asked and the three men shrugged their shoulders. Thurman covered his mouth and coughed. Harjunpaa jumped over the path and headed down the slope.

The distance was short but all the same Harjunpaa was out of breath by the time he reached the water; it was hard to try and avoid stepping where somebody else before him might have trodden. The smell of the sea was far more pungent here; it stank of mud and rotting bits of wood, and the metallic smell of blood was almost obscured. Harjunpaa squatted, sending hordes of flies up. The sun was suddenly extraordinarily hot on his neck and on his back.

The face was covered in wounds. They were all relatively small and not deadly as such—unless there had been excessive bleeding. He examined the shirt but could find no knife wounds, at least not on the side he could see. The neck seemed unbroken. Harjunpaa didn't know what to think; a broken skull was another possibility but that might not be certain before an autopsy was performed.

He touched the bare arm and was startled.

The skin was warm.

He lifted the arm. It bent easily, there was no stiffness and the underside was quite pale; there was not even the smallest telltale sign of burst blood vessels. Harjunpaa gasped. His pulse was racing. Kneeling down, he pressed his ear close to the man's face. He could detect wheezing, barely audible breathing.

Harjunpaa sprang up, lost his balance and stepped into the sea, without noticing. He swayed back and forth for a while, senselessly opening and clenching his fists. "He's alive!"

His shout was harsh and loud. The seagulls left the

water without a sound and a cloud of sparrows scattered out of the bushes.

The others stood still; only Thurman bent down, reaching forward.

"Don't talk rubbish."

"He's alive!" Harjunpaa repeated. "He's warm, he's breathing—he's alive! Get an ambulance quick. And a doctor!"

Thurman jumped up and rushed through the shrubbery to the car. Soon they could hear him shouting into the radio, "Aleksi . . . what the hell's it called now . . . Central! This is 8-9-1 calling!"

"Help me, someone!" Harjunpaa shouted. "We must get him into a better position, up on the path."

Harko was already on his way down, scattering stones as he came.

"You grab him under the arms. We must get him into a better position, whatever there might be on his back . . . this way he'll suffocate."

"Lift by the knees, Timo."

"Can't do it . . . there is something."

Harjunpaa could not get hold of the legs, he could not pull the legs apart, they were somehow stuck together. He went in deeper and raised the legs up together. Harko slipped his hands under the arms, grabbed the wrists and lifted with infinite care.

"Ready."

"Bloody hell, bloody hell," Lofman kept mumbling somewhere nearby.

Moving was difficult when there was no way of seeing where to step; feet slipped on smooth stones, shoes got stuck in holes. The body felt exceptionally heavy. Even though they were both experienced, having taken down dozens of men who had hanged themselves, still both were panting and sweating by the time they reached the path.

"Over there, on the grass."

"Fire station ambulance is on its way!"

"Turn him sideways. No, not like that . . . put his arm under . . ."

"Let me! Out of the way . . . get me something to put under his head!"

They maneuvered the man into a first-aid position of sorts and Harjunpaa knelt down. His fingers fumbled uncertainly, as if they no longer knew what to do. Then he gritted his teeth and probed the man's mouth with his finger, the same way he had learned to search for a bullet-hole in the mouth. There was nothing untoward, and the tongue was in the right position. A thin trickle of blood ran out of the mouth. Harjunpaa unbuckled the man's belt—his belly was oddly distended, tight. Harjunpaa could not imagine why that should be.

Harjunpaa stood up and rubbed his brow. Only now, when there was a lull and the rush seemed deceptively to be over, he noticed how his feet and hands were shaking; even his teeth were chattering. He made an effort to take a slow deep breath, looking at the man lying limply on the ground. A name of a clothes shop was printed on the front of the white shirt: A MAN OF HIS TIME. Harjunpaa turned to face the sea. Somehow he knew that although the man was still breathing, it was nothing but a reflex.

He heard a car door bang and somebody pushing through the shrubbery.

"For heaven's sake," somebody said, it had to be Bergman, the voice was the same as over the car radio. "What on earth . . . why did I send that kid to take a look? . . . I thought it would teach him his job." Harjunpaa moved quickly away but he could still hear Bergman's voice. "Whoever's done it, who could do a thing like that, they should all be tied together and shot."

He was no longer pretending, there was an impotent rage in his voice. The wailing of sirens reached them from somewhere far beyond the railway yard.

3

Mikael awoke to the rattle of coat hangers—father had returned. He propped himself up on an elbow, rubbed his face, and fought against the sleep that was dragging his head back to the pillow, like a weight. But a part of him was awake already; in the depths of his mind there was apprehension: Something dreadful was about to happen or had happened already. Only he couldn't think what. He blinked hard, still he couldn't remember. But he knew it was important to know whether his father was in a good mood or not.

Mikael held his breath, listening.

That thud meant that the newspaper was thrown on the table in the foyer.

What usually followed was that Sod sat on a low stool, grunted, and pulled his boots off. He always wore boots, even in summer. His socks were smelly. And he wore jodhpurs even though no one else in the force wore them any longer. And when he finished work he only changed his jacket, so that every soul in the neighborhood knew what he was, Sod with his floppy jodhpurs and his creaking boots.

"Your dad's a pig," they would say to Mikael. Since Jani died he had felt even lonelier than before.

But now Sod did not sit down. Instead he creaked straight to the kitchen and to the refrigerator, took out a can of beer, opened it—Mikael could hear the hiss—and

19

drank, still not sitting down. He could gulp a whole can down without drawing breath, his adam's apple pumping.

Mikael curled his toes slowly. The feeling of unease became stronger still; the last time Sod had gone directly to the refrigerator had been some time in the spring. By nightfall he had been mad and had given mum such a black eye she had been too ashamed to go to work.

Mikael heard Sod plunk the empty beer can on the sink and burp. And open the refrigerator again!

Mikael sat up, twisting his fingers.

From downstairs came the sharp sound of metal against glass, then two short gulps, and finally a grunt.

That had been the vodka bottle. Sod had to be in a really vile mood. Bedclothes rustled next door, so mother was awake, too, and didn't want to go downstairs.

Mikael put his thumb into his mouth and chewed the nail, already bitten down.

Now Sod kicked his boots off and rattled his keys. He was going to the small room that was always locked; even mother had no business there. Sod called it his office but he never did anything in there, except clean the guns he kept there. He was a keen hunter, he could shoot anything, and if any moose strayed into town he would be called, even from home, to shoot it. He took all his holidays in the autumn, to be able to go shooting. He never took Mikael along, not that he complained, it was far nicer at home when his father was away. Even mother was different.

Sod always locked his service gun in its cupboard and relocked the door.

Next he would have a smoke and then he would come upstairs. He never ate anything after working nights, only drank some beer, and then tried to get some sleep but usually couldn't—he was on nights every fourth day and his system had got messed up. Mother *could* sleep after working nights. She worked in a hospital as an auxiliary nurse, and was on every night one week and off all the next week.

The smell of cigarettes wafted upstairs.

Sod was kicking furniture as he paced up and down with a quick, ill-tempered step; he must be really mad about something. Now he picked up the phone and dialed. Mikael counted the digits, eight of them. It had to be a direct line to the station.

"Can you find Hoglund for me," Sod grunted to the mouthpiece, and waited. Finally Hoglund or someone else came, for he said, "It's Bergman, morning. I should report in tomorrow at six, for patrol. But you better start looking for a replacement. Yes, I know it's Sunday rate but my back doesn't. I've got such bloody pain I don't know which way to turn. It's all that sitting in the car. I'll go and see a doc first thing on Monday morning if it doesn't clear by then."

He put the receiver down, muttering, "Bloody berk!"

There was nothing wrong with Sod's back. It had been x-rayed and tractioned, he had been in the hospital many times for it, but nothing wrong could be found apart from some wearing out. Still it always gave him trouble if he had had a row at work or if the nearby restaurant needed him to help out. He had tried to wheedle an early pension out of his back, but without success.

He went to the refrigerator once more before the stairs creaked.

Mikael lay down quickly and pulled the covers over his head. He bit his lip in order to stop his heart from beating so loudly—then he remembered he hadn't shut his door properly: It was still ajar. He stiffened and could barely make his breathing sound normal.

Sod passed his room—he never came in, anyway—and went straight to their bedroom, shutting the door. That didn't make any difference since Mikael's bed was next to the partition wall. He had moved his bed there when

21

Jani's things had been taken away. It felt better this way, when he was in his room in the daytime and mum was sleeping next door, on the other side of the wall. It was almost as if he was next to her.

Sod was probably getting undressed, pulling at his clothes. Mother didn't say anything, probably feigning sleep.

"Bloody hell, can't even get buttons sewn on properly."

The bed creaked as if mother was sitting up.

"What's up?" Her voice was neutral to minimize risking an outburst.

"What do you mean?"

"Well, I thought—"

"Better not even try."

Sod grumbled on but Mikael couldn't make out what he said. He unbuckled his belt, the brass buckle clanked. Then he sat heavily down on the bed.

Suddenly Sod was raving, "What is it coming to . . . they take on complete novices. They have tests and examinations—and God knows what else! They know nothing, they can do nothing. They can't tell who's drunk and who's sober, they can't even tell the dead from the living. And who has to take the rap when they mess it up?"

"What is it now?"

"It's the same shit year in year out!"

Some clothing hit the floor and Sod threw himself down. Mikael knew what he would look like lying there, on his back, legs apart, one fist over his forehead.

Mother made to get up but Sod said, "Don't go."

Mother: "You'd sleep better."

Sod: "Come here."

Mother: "Not just now. I'm not in the mood. And Miku."

Sod: "But I am. Come on . . . there."

The bed creaked when Sod pulled mother down and heaved himself over to her side. Sod grunted a few times before he got in. Mikael had sneaked to the door once or twice to have a look: mother with her legs up, round bottom showing under Sod who was pumping on her, underpants halfway down his thighs. Now he was panting. There was no sound from mother.

Mikael felt his penis move.

He covered it with his hand and squeezed, closed his eyes, and thought about Ulla.

Only he couldn't remember her clearly, he couldn't even remember her face.

At the back of his mind there was a big dark lump. It radiated something threatening, revolting, something that made his stomach turn. He no longer could imagine anything, he pulled his hands up to cover his ears.

How he hated everyone, even his mother!

She always gave in, never stood up for herself. She didn't even stand up for him, instead she always nagged and complained, "Don't do that, father'll be angry, I'll tell him, be quiet now and don't disturb your father." And yet she was far younger than Sod, at least fifteen years younger; she could have told Sod to stuff it, and take himself off, even get married to someone else. But she never did anything, didn't even hint at divorce. All she did was have rows with Sod, let him beat her up, and open her legs.

Mikael rolled on to his belly; he couldn't help the sobs that shook him.

The next think he knew, there was clatter in the upstairs toilet, followed by cursing.

Then he remembered, every smallest detail—or rather, it had been on his mind all the time, really, only he had not remembered that it was there. The recollection sloshed his belly with icy water: Sod had fallen over the bucket Mikael had left in the bathroom. The bucket contained water, plenty of detergent, and his jeans.

"Who the hell left this bucket lying about?"

"Oh, no, water all over the place."

"Why d'you leave it there?"

"I didn't. Those are Miku's jeans."

"And since when has he washed his own clothes?"

"Well, they weren't here when I went to bed last night."

Until then Sod's voice had been crackling with rage; now it went very cold and quiet. "I see."

But he was still mad, and tried to find reasons why he should be madder still. Mikael knew how his face was twitching now, and his feet stomping.

"In other words . . . the boy came in so late you don't even know how late. I'm not having him messing about with those louts. They drink—hell knows what they do—I bet he's been sick all over his trousers. I'm not having him go the same way as his brother. I'm going to put a stop to that right now."

Sod was coming. Mikael pulled the covers over his head, whispered anxiously, "Jani."

Jani had been tall and strong, different. Once he had given Sod such a punch in the guts that he had fallen down. After that Sod had not dared even to threaten Jani. Well, first he'd said that he'd shoot himself, but Jani only laughed and said, "Why don't you," and that was that.

The covers were ripped off.

Sod was standing by the bedside in his underpants—his fat belly was sticking out and tufts of yellowish hair protruded through the holes in his string vest.

"Where were you last night?" he demanded, angry spots burning on his cheeks and his eyes somehow clouded. He raised his arm; it was a thick arm, full of freckles. The fist at the end looked oddly small.

"Fuck off," shouted Mikael. "Fuck off, you pig!"

Sod's mouth fell open. He said nothing but his breath-

24

ing became heavy, and then he rushed out of the room—
he was getting his belt. Mother was trying to mollify him,
"Nils . . . Father! Dear Nils."

Mikael could feel the floor shaking. He grabbed the
sides of his bed and kicked about wildly.

"I wish you'd be killed," he yelled. "Killed!"

4

"Can 8-9-1 hear 8-2-4 direct?" Harjunpaa was prepared for a lengthy wait. Although he was sure that the police car was still parked in the opening close to the water, he was also sure that it would be empty and that all the men—Norri, Harko, Thurman, and Ketonen from the technical department who had joined the team later that morning—would be combing the shrubbery and the footpath, within hearing distance but not realizing that a call for 8-9-1 was meant for them. Harjunpaa rested his head on the back of the seat and allowed the microphone to slide down to his lap. He had left the car door open and the sun shone very warmly on his feet on the cobblestones. The bottoms of his trouser legs were nearly dry. He had no socks, only sandals, down at heel, borrowed from the duty officer.

"8-9-1, can you hear me?"

Harjunpaa was outside the hospital. Next to him on the front seat was a plastic bag, misting on the inside, which contained the clothes Taisto Nilsson had worn. Topmost on the pile were the shoes. On Harjunpaa's lap lay a much smaller bag that contained a pigskin wallet, some personal documents, a few bank notes, and a restaurant bill for the Old Cellar, totaling nearly 300 marks, with yesterday's date. Just behind the police Lada was the old hospital, with its timber pillars and small, pitched roofs. In one of its operating theaters all the bright lights were at this very moment focused on Taisto Nilsson, who

26

himself knew nothing of the feverish battle to keep him alive. Harjunpaa glanced at his watch—half-past nine already. Behind the iron railings he could see people walking leisurely down the street, on their way to the market, or the zoo—wherever it was that people went on a summer Saturday.

"Harjunpaa calling for Norri or Harko."

This time he didn't have to wait more than ten seconds.

"Norri is receiving in Kaisaniemi."

Harjunpaa's face grew less tense; in his mind's eye he could see Norri as he stood there, next to the police car, in his made-to-measure suit, holding the microphone and outwardly cool, although embarrassed by the crowds staring at him behind the roped-off area.

"Are we being overheard?"

"I'll turn the volume down," Norri said. "Go ahead."

"They're still operating so we don't know for sure. In any case it's critical. I got the impression that internal bleeding was so extensive that it could have caused brain damage."

Norri didn't reply at once. Harjunpaa shifted his position uneasily; he had wondered if it was in order to call Norri in.

"Did you manage to get his shoes as they were?" There was no discernible criticism in Norri's voice.

"Yes, I did. No question it was deliberate. The shoes were tied together, knot by knot."

Norri was silent for a long moment. Then he spoke in a low voice, "The growing impression we're getting here is that they were youngsters . . ."

Harjunpaa waited for Norri to go on, but when the silence continued he said: "He's unmarried, lives with his mother in Eira, works as a caretaker in a house in Huvilakatu. I think maybe I should go there now—"

"Yes, you do that," cut in Norri promptly. "You can go

27

straight to the station from there, we'll be finished here shortly."

Harjunpaa's face went blank. Unconsciously he had been hoping—against hope—that Norri would ask him to do something else instead. Then he cleared his throat, started the car, and closed the door, shutting out the smell of roses and scattering the sparrows that had been picking dead insects from the car grille.

Houses on Huvilakatu were low-built, and pretty reminiscent of a small English town. A warm reflection moved at the back of Harjunpaa's mind, in spite of the apprehension he felt. When Pauliina was a baby and they still lived in town, they often came here for their Sunday morning walk. They used to say Huvilakatu was so nice only happy people could live there.

The house Harjunpaa was looking for was not on the sunny side. It was dark brown and taller than its neighbors.

Access to the caretaker's flat was direct from the street, three steps down. To the right of the door was a window, with a colorful display of flowers and plants. A white cat was sleeping among the flowerpots.

Harjunpaa stood at the door, his head bowed, as if about to nod off. Somehow he felt it would have been easier to come and say Taisto was dead, not that he was neither dead nor alive. He felt it would be more merciful without this useless splinter of hope, easier to accept the loss and to face the sheer sorrow.

Before Harjunpaa could ring the bell the door opened. Taisto Nilsson's mother was short and round; she reached only halfway up Harjunpaa's chest. She had white hair and a wrinkled face, an old woman, well over seventy by the look of her. But her eyes were bright and intelligent; somehow you knew she could understand where others remained ignorant.

"Good morning," she said, slowly, and studied her visitor from top to toe. It wasn't an embarrassing inspection, more like a handshake.

"Good morning. I'm Detective Inspector Harjunpaa from the SUOPO. I presume you are Mrs. Nilsson. Taisto's mother."

"Yes. But good heavens, I'm keeping you outside. Please come in." She was not scared in the way people usually were, but she became oddly busy all of a sudden, darting, waving her hand about as if she had just burned it on the stove.

The home was cramped and quite dark, neat as a pin, old-fashioned, harking back to times past. The furniture was heavy and dark, covered with antimacassars and ornaments. On the walls were framed photographs and wall hangings, a stuffed moose head, a green felt hat with a pheasant's feather hanging from one of its horns.

"Sit down, please, take a seat."

"Thanks," Harjunpaa remained standing. "It's about Taisto, your son."

"Taisto, yes, yes . . . I guessed something like that . . . poor boy, when he gets drunk . . . but he is such a nice boy, never a bad word to his mother. . . ."

She was talking fast, almost breathlessly, flitting around the room with small steps. She straightened a tablecloth here, picked something up over there, chased the cat off the windowsill. Now she would not look at Harjunpaa.

"Mrs. Nilsson . . ."

"Taisto became caretaker here when his father died. He does all the work, he scrubs the stairs and all. Daytime he works in the shipyard, he's a plumber—he nips home most lunchbreaks, to see I'm all right. Never married, our Taisto, keeps saying that there's time for that later. And where would I go. . . . All his money he brings home. He does get drunk on weekends but where's the harm in that?"

Harjunpaa closed his eyes for a minute; the sleepless

29

night was suddenly making itself felt. Tiredness spread like some heavy liquid through his limbs, dulled all sense. He guessed that the old woman was building a fence around herself, to stop him saying what he had to say. Somewhere in his tired mind he knew he shouldn't leave her alone once he had finished with his business here, only he couldn't for the time being think how to organize someone to look after her.

"I am sorry but I have to . . ."

"Coffee! You must have a cup of coffee . . . why didn't I think. . . . It's all ready. I have some sandwiches made here. You must eat something, you're so skinny."

With a slow and heavy step Harjunpaa followed the old woman to her kitchen.

Along one wall was a bed, all made up. On a hook by the door hung a man's brown cardigan, the sleeves elaborately darned; next to it was a pair of blue overalls; on the floor a pair of boots and slippers.

Harjunpaa sat at the table, already set for two, and stared at the small bubbles of air that floated across his coffee. He did not want any of the sandwiches that had been made for Taisto whose face was black with bleeding, his belly bloated with blood; in his lunch break Taisto would nip home to see that all was well with mother.

Out of the corner of his eye Harjunpaa saw the cat sneaking into the kitchen, saw it jump up and curl in the old woman's lap. That's better, he thought, not so lonely. He knew he had waited far too long already and looked up.

The old woman was stroking her cat and crying.

"I knew it at once," she whispered, barely audible. "I saw it in your eyes—he's dead, my Taisto."

5

Mikael sneaked down the stairs as quietly as possible.

The hall was dark. He stood still, holding his breath and listening.

Mother was in the kitchen. You could tell she was ironing by the smell, a nice, warm smell—and also because she was humming. Sod wasn't in; he'd left for his doorman's job at six.

Mikael bent down, slowly, trying to keep his legs apart, but still a small moan escaped. He groped under the coat stand. His fingers touched his father's boots and pulled away instantly; then he found his own pair. He stood up, clutching his boots; he'd come down only in order to fetch them, otherwise he would have gone straight from his room, over the balcony railing, and onto the tree outside.

Now he was ready to go.

And yet something was holding him back.

Holding the wall with one hand he leaned forward far enough to see into the kitchen. The light was on and he could see the whole room clearly. Mother was standing with her back to him; she wore only a pair of knickers and a bra and somehow that made her look quite vulnerable. Nobody—at least no strangers—should see her like that, with her bottom so broad and sort of lumpy. Her hair, too, was stringy. It always was when she had her week off. She was quite pathetic, really.

Mikael sniffed. For a brief moment he wanted to go in,

touch his mother's bare back, and say, "Hi!" It was all because of that smell; if he closed his eyes it made him feel like a baby again, playing with his toy cars under the ironing board while she was ironing.

"Shit."

Mikael tiptoed to the door that led to the small room. His heart beat faster. He knew the room was crammed full of guns—there were at least three different rifles and four shotguns on the wall; in the cupboard there was a Parabellum and an FN—and at least one revolver with a barrel so wide he could push his finger in. He turned the handle lightly but the door was locked, just as he had expected. It always was locked. But the gap between the door and the frame was wide enough to take a blade from his pocket knife. He would try it sometime, he decided.

He sneaked to the small foyer between the outside door and the hall and quietly closed the inside door after him. He had to leave the front door unlocked, it couldn't be closed without noise. Not that it would have mattered even if mother had caught him sneaking out. All she ever did was nag and shout. It was different with Sod, all this had been his idea: that Mikael had to stay in for a week. As some sort of punishment. For what? It would be a good solution if Sod shot his own head off.

A moment later Mikael had reached the playing fields behind the row of houses. From the fields you could see into the kitchen and the drawing room, but Mikael did not turn to look. He headed away across the fields, walking slowly, legs still slightly apart—although now they only hurt if they rubbed together. Step by step he felt he was shedding weight; he no longer felt bad about leaving, he was glad to be gone. No longer did he fear that Sod would suddenly rush after him—and as for mother, well, it was her own fault for being so pathetic.

He could have done with a smoke—or a beer. He

wanted to get a bit drunk really, he felt he deserved it, it was owed to him. Leo would have both cigarettes and beer, sometimes he even had wine. He knew how to get it from the men who visited his mother. Leo wasn't likely to be angry any longer; he was so prickly that most people were afraid of him and he was on his own. Most days he lounged around his home, if his mother wasn't in, or tinkered with his moped or paddled around in the cave. Sometimes he hung around with the bums in the woods—occasionally when on his own he could play like a kid, even though he was so old. Mikael walked faster. He knew he would find Leo sooner or later—or rather, Leo would find him.

Mikael came to the footpath that ran along the far side of the field. He slowed down. Beyond the path was a small copse and beyond that he could see some low-rise flats. These were altogether different from most houses in Kontula; even the people who lived there were somehow different. That's where Ulla lived, in the house nearest to him. Mikael did not walk down the footpath after all; instead he climbed the low hill toward the houses, making his way through birches and aspen.

Ulla was no girl but a grown-up, at least thirty but no more. It was quite odd that they had become friends—or whatever it was they were. Mikael wasn't quite sure.

They had first met on the previous New Year's Eve. Mikael had been on his way to meet Leo and had no booze. Then he had spotted three bottles of white wine on a low balcony. They had been put out to cool in the snow. Light shone through the windows but nobody had been about when Mikael had climbed up. He had already stuffed the first bottle inside his jacket when a voice behind him said, "Hey! You!"

That had been Ulla. It had been her balcony and her flat and her wine. But she never had said anything, only looked at him, her head slightly to one side, while he put

33

the bottles back. She had let him go, hadn't laughed at him or anything. And then, later, when he was walking past she had been hanging clothes on the balcony and had said hello. That's how they had become mates or whatever, and Mikael liked to drop in occasionally, even though she never gave him any booze. Leo said she was a whore, but that was because he was envious.

Mikael could see light behind the curtains; his breathing became faster. Ulla was not often home in the evening, more often in the daytime. Mikael picked up a pebble and chucked it over the balcony, at the window. It made a nice sharp sound. He waited but nothing happened. He threw another and waited again. This time the curtain was swished aside—everything Ulla did looked very prompt—and there she was standing at the window, her head tilted as on that first night. She let go of the curtain and opened the door to the balcony but did not come out.

"Hi," she said, and by the tone Mikael could tell that she was busy—or annoyed. "Look, I'm just about to go out. I'm in a tearing hurry. . . ."

Mikael didn't reply. He couldn't move his lips and his chest felt heavy. He lowered his eyes and scraped the tarmac slowly with one foot. Ulla opened her mouth, changed her mind, and said quickly, "OK. Come in while I get ready."

Mikael heaved himself up to the balcony and went in.

Ulla's home was muted. All colors were pale, creamy, and there were hairy rugs and round leather cushions with camels painted on them. It also smelled nice, not of perfume but something like it. She always had some quiet music on, now it was some violin or something.

"Why don't you sit here," said Ulla. "I have to do my face. Got a sudden invitation, out of the blue."

"Thanks," mumbled Mikael, staring at his hands. Ulla moved toward her bedroom but paused in the doorway.

34

"How come you're out at this hour?" She didn't ask in a mean way, as adults usually did, she asked because she wanted to know.

"I was just going home," Mikael lied. Ulla left it there, she was smart. She walked quickly to her dressing table and sat on the stool.

Mikael moved to the other end of the sofa so that he could see into the bedroom. Only now did he dare look at her; he always became so shy when she was near, stupidly shy. All he could do was to stare at the floor and in her presence he could never think of anything clever to say, instead he almost stuttered. It was easier like this, when they were in separate rooms.

Ulla was brushing something on her cheeks. Sitting down she looked almost short—and yet she had long, slim arms and legs; slender fingers too, with dark red nails. Her buttocks on the stool were excitingly round when seen from behind, like now. Her breasts weren't particularly large, just big enough to move about when she walked. She had black hair; she dyed it black. She was wearing a white slip with a nice shine to it. You could tell she had no bra on since only one set of straps crossed the shoulders. But she had knickers, you could see them through the slip.

Mikael felt his face grow hot. He was blushing more and more, as if something red was seeping through his skin. He never thought about it when he was in her flat, but when he was alone at home at night and the house was empty and quiet, then he might think of her and put his hand under the blankets and stroke. And it felt good and he would finish himself off. But then, when he saw Ulla again, he felt ashamed and it was difficult to meet her eye, as if she could tell by the way he looked.

"What have you been up to?" You could tell from her voice she wasn't all that interested but was nice enough to ask.

35

"Not a lot," Mikael said, his voice thick. But since that sounded so dull he quickly added: "But I did kill a man."

"Please, don't," said Ulla, shaking her round shoulders as if chilled. But at the same time she sort of laughed.

"No, it's true. I asked him, quite nicely, you know, if he had a bottle-opener. But he started talking shit, all about kids not being allowed to drink. So we got mad and I killed him. Buried him under stones in the middle of the station so that all the dogs would piss on him forever, deserves it, stupid berk like that. I took his falsies and his watch. I meant to give them to you, as a present. But since he was such a shit I just threw them away."

Ulla was amused, she was chuckling quietly. Then she put something down on the table and turned to look to the other room.

"Why d'you always talk like that?" She was quite serious now, but added less heavily, "And you really shouldn't drink, you know. At your age the liver cannot cope with alcohol."

"Mine can. And anyway, I don't drink all that much. Only enough to give things a spin."

"Why?"

"Well, you must do something to have some fun. And when you're a bit drunk you don't think about all the shit."

"Yes, yes. You really think you know it all."

She turned back to face the table and started on her nails. The varnish had a nice smell; it made you think of Christmas in the middle of summer.

Mikael stood up and stretched. He hadn't meant to move but somehow he ended up at the bedroom door, leaning on the frame. The smell in the bedroom was even stronger than elsewhere in the flat. It made you feel you were very close to another person, smelling her skin. A dress was spread on the bed; Ulla was obviously going to wear it tonight. It seemed so thin that it had to be almost transparent. That did not feel nice. It wasn't right that any shit could see how nice she looked, see her bottom and thighs and even her nipples if they went hard. Mikael took a deep breath, thinking that soon Ulla would leave, go to see some man, and then he, too, would have to go—back home if he didn't manage to find Leo.

"Want to see something?" His voice shook a bit. Ulla looked at him through the mirror and nodded. Mikael moved closer—so close that he could see Ulla's spine disappear in a neat line of bumps down her back. It would have been nice to run a finger down those bumps, one by one—but he didn't. Instead he hoisted his trouser leg up, exposing half his calf.

"See."

Ulla glanced down quickly and said nothing. Then she realized what she had seen and went stiff. She put the bottle of nail varnish down and turned around.

"What on earth has happened to you?"

"I told you there was a fight."

Mikael lifted his leg. The calf was patterned across with swollen, dark bruises, one next to the other. Just beneath the knee, where the buckle had caught him, were two rough, five-inch wounds. Left on their own they had started to fester.

Mikael looked up. It was the first time her face had ever been so near. She was pale, with wide, shocked eyes, her mouth was open and her lips trembled visibly. Mikael sobbed. He found it hard to believe that Ulla would look like that because of him. He looked down again, sniffing, and tried to fight against the feeling of suffocation that was welling up. But it was no good, his shoulders began to heave and the next moment he was sniveling, eyes blinded with tears.

"How did this happen? Miku, you must tell me." Mikael felt Ulla's hand in his, was led toward the bed.

"Take your trousers off," she ordered.

"No."

"Take them off."

His belt was unbuckled, his jeans pulled down. Ulla forced him to sit. He was so ashamed he had to grit his teeth. But he didn't fight her. Instead he gave in to his tears, keeled over, and lay limp.

He could hear Ulla's voice tremble, "Oh, dear God."

Mikael lay there, staring at the ceiling. There were no fresh tears now, only the aftermath, occasional sobs. In a way he felt easier now, as if after a long, restful night, or as if things had somehow taken a turn for the better. And Ulla's fingers smoothed cream on his leg, soft and light, never hurting even when they went over the open wounds.

"Who was it?" Her voice was quite normal, not angry or anything.

"Father."

"Your own father?"

"Yes, he had a belt."

"And where was your mother?"

"At home. She was standing at the door."

"And didn't do anything? She should have called the police."

Mikael felt the lump in his throat again and had to bat his eyelids rapidly. "She can't," he said with difficulty. "He *is* a policeman. If she called help he might get the sack. What could we live on? I don't think she's paid all that much."

"Jesus." Ulla was quiet. Then she put the tube of cream on the bedside table and went to turn the music up. She had never before had anything on so loud.

Mikael didn't get up at once. He was thinking how nice it would be if Ulla was his mother.

Half an hour later it was already quite dark. Mikael walked along the footpath toward the pond, the playing fields on his other side. He walked slowly, with his hands in his pockets, and dragging his feet on the ground. Crying had made him feel different, the dark lump that had lain at the back of his mind all day had gone, and also gone was the malicious delight of having sneaked away from home. Now he felt flat; in an obscure way he felt a craving for something that didn't exist.

"Miku!"

Mikael stopped in his tracks. It was Leo, sitting on a giant frog made from twisted tree trunks. Now he jumped down and strolled up to Mikael, wobbling on legs like strands of boiled macaroni.

"Hi."

A cigarette dangled from Leo's mouth, almost finished. He took a hasty drag from it and passed it on to Mikael, who put the butt to his lips without looking at Leo. He thought that Leo, too, was not looking at him.

Silently they drifted in the direction of Leo's building. It was big, both tall and long. There had to be hundreds of flats in it, all belonging to the city council. The walls were scrawled with graffiti.

"A pane of glass in your staircase is broken." Mikael thought it sounded silly but it was better than not saying anything at all.

"Guess who smashed it."

"You?"

"Yep. The other night. I left my keys behind. I was standing here, waiting. I must have waited ten hours at least and nobody came. So I yelled for a key. I shouted so hard I thought my head would split. I shouted that I was all alone and had nowhere to go. But none of those shits would chuck a key down, they never do. And all the time I know the house is full of them, shitting in their beds, and that they'd heard me and still did nothing. So I picked this huge stone and smashed it through the

39

bloody door. You should've been here . . . the noise! . . . the glass all over the place."

"Never."

"Yep. Like it was raining ice or something. I bet they'll report it to the police or something. They all hate me, every cow in this building hates me. Let them, who cares. I don't give a shit."

They stared at the door. Mikael felt they were at it for too long, that the silence was becoming oppressive. He shifted his feet, opened his mouth but shut it again.

"I wonder how that bloke is," he said suddenly.

"What bloody bloke?"

Leo was baffled, his eyes uncomprehending. Mikael felt his face grow hot again.

"Well," he said in a thick voice, "the one in town last night."

"Oh, that . . . how the hell would I know? All I know is he sure fell flat on his face once he tried to walk away. Sure thing. I tied his shoelaces together so many times they couldn't ever come undone."

"Yeah."

Mikael was blushing more than ever. Why couldn't Leo ever understand what was being said. He knew he wouldn't get his voice right, but still he had to try. "What I mean is . . . do you think he was hurt?"

"Hurt? Oh fuck off, a berk like that! Besides, he started it all, mouthing off like that. And he was bigger than us—it was his own fault. And what's it to do with you? It's his problem if he was hurt or not."

"You sure?"

Leo stopped, resting his hands on his hips. You could tell by his expression that he was getting mad.

"What the hell are you on about? I bloody bet he's this very minute swilling beer somewhere. Or mouthing off to someone else, like to us last night."

"Yes." Mikael swallowed, looking at Leo, imagining

40

how the man was drinking from a beer glass, wiping froth from his mouth. "Sure. What the hell, sure." He laughed, it felt good to laugh.

"I wish Lauri would be back home soon," Leo said when they drew closer to the shopping center. "We could go and see videos at his place. His father has brought some bril videos from Sweden. I've seen them at least a thousand times. There's this ace one, they chase this bird and get her and hang her on a meat hook—she screams and kicks, see. And then they take a chainsaw to her. . . . Wrumm! . . . And in the other one they smash loads and loads of cars. There's this one driver, racer or something, his car is magic. You see this guy's face all the time when they chase him, but they never catch him, not him. I want to drive like that . . . flat out. I wouldn't give a shit, my car would go straight through, crash through everything. . . ."

Mikael felt himself responding, although mildly. He tried to egg himself on, he felt he had to get enthusiastic, if only for Leo's sake. He stretched out his arms as if holding a steering wheel.

"We're off . . . wruum . . . foot down. Yahoo!"

Mikael stopped, his arms falling to his sides as if he had just realized something. His eyes focused somewhere beyond Leo and he sounded like a sleepwalker when he said: "Think. If Sod was on duty . . . he'd stop us and pull the door open. I'd step out and he'd take his gun, cock it . . . click! And then he'd shoot. Straight through my chest . . . through my heart . . . I'd fall . . . like this."

Mikael pressed his hands on his chest, fell slowly on his knees, and rolled over onto his side. The tarmac was hard, small flints dug into his cheek, but he didn't move; it was good to lie like this, unthinking.

He was kicked on the shin.

"Get up, idiot." Leo sounded distant. "Listen! I know a Ford Anglia in a parking lot in Keinutie. We'll go take a

41

look. There's no wheel lock, nothing on it. Hell, get up now."

Mikael sat up. His face was wet under the eyes and on the cheeks.

"Only then he'd realize it's me," he whispered. "But I'd be dead. However much he'd cry . . . I'd be dead."

6

"Well, that's it." Monica sounded so peeved that Harjunpaa turned to look at her. The lights from the restaurant left her face in shadow, so he couldn't see her expression, but Harjunpaa could guess that her mouth was in a tight pout. Monica had gathered her hair up in a loose knot, and during the evening, strands had come free and now, with the bright lights behind her, they surrounded her head like a frosty halo.

Harjunpaa sighed in agreement. He was probably even more annoyed than Monica, he had known from the start that it would be pointless to question anybody but the staff in the restaurant. But since that had produced no better results than anything else this futile Sunday, he had decided to have a go on the customers anyway. And it had been a mistake.

People had either been drunk or could neither hear nor understand the questions put to them. Least of all had they been willing to understand why they should look at a photograph of a fair-haired man.

"That's Pena's brother . . . Pena, this bloke's got your brother's photograph."

And chaos had descended when a fat man, sitting next to the door, grabbed Monica and pulled her onto his lap. Monica and Harjunpaa left the place swiftly, to the accompaniment of breaking crockery, as the fat man fell from his chair.

"Monica," Harjunpaa asked when they were out of ear-shot, "did you do it on purpose?"

Monica chuckled quietly. "Do you think anyone noticed?"

"I shouldn't think so, it was so quick." And suddenly, without any particular reason, Harjunpaa felt confident the case would be solved. He no longer felt it had been a waste of time to come where Nilsson most likely had been on Friday night, or that it might have been more profitable to stay near the railway station where Harko and Wallender were talking to people hanging around. Harjunpaa glanced at his watch; it was almost eleven already. The sky was deep blue, turning black, and the undergrowth and shrubbery in the park were looking very dark. Silently they headed in the direction of the National Theater where their Lada was parked.

On Saturday Norri had roped in Monica and Wallender to work on the case, and they had managed to get through quite a lot in a relatively short time. People living nearby had been interviewed, as had the staffs of nearby restaurants. Nilsson had spent Friday night in the area with three of his mates. Two of these had already been traced and questioned. All the relevant police reports for Friday had been checked. The most likely route for Nilsson to have taken had been gone through with a fine-tooth comb, including all the hot-dog stands on the way. Notice boards at the nearby railway engineering works and on the jetties by the bay had got a police notice asking for information concerning Friday night's events.

But nothing tangible had emerged. They didn't have even a rough idea of what the culprits looked like. The clues collected from the scene of the crime were almost as meager: There was a footprint that might have come from an ordinary jogging shoe, not necessarily worn by the assailant; there were a few smudged fingerprints on a broken beer bottle—nothing good enough to be of any

44

use for the criminal records people. But they would be good enough for identification if a suspect was found.

The police were not on a murder hunt, not yet, at any rate, but all the same Norri was putting on the pressure. It seemed that Nilsson had been knocked down with a blow from a beer bottle. After that somebody had jumped on his chest and his belly had been pounded with a mass of heavy stones. These had caused severe rupturing in almost all his internal organs. At any moment the case might become a murder. Blood was sloshing around, the surgeon had told Norri. "And I have to admit that a couple of times I hoped he would die on the operating table."

They reached the Kaisaniemi fields. As a schoolboy, Harjunpaa had played baseball there. He would have preferred not to remember: Memories made him feel anxious, maybe because he never could hit the ball.

"It's odd to think that right now they might be hanging around somewhere near," he said, then quickly added an opinion that had been voiced umpteen times before: "But it's certain that they must be quite young. This case has too many similarities with the train tunnel case and with the Veräjämäki murder . . . wasn't one of the train tunnel boys barely twelve?"

"I wish they *would* hang round here," Monica said. "The trouble is that round the station you find kids from every corner of the town. Our boys might be sitting in some suburb right now, watching telly with mum and dad."

"I know," Harjunpaa said. There was nothing else to say. Gravel crunched underfoot, the distant rumble of a train came from the railway sidings nearby, and from further away, from behind the trees, came the constant hum of the city.

They were now in the darkest part of the park. Birches formed a tall, opaque wall, and any remaining streetlights were just blue spots amid the branches. On the left, where the tennis courts were, somebody giggled hysterically. Somewhere else, much closer by, a bottle was broken, bushes rustled, someone cursed. Harjunpaa's palms were sweating, he knew they were in the middle of the worst spot for muggings in the whole of Helsinki, and he also knew that being together did not offer them any real security. Neither did the gun each was carrying. He stole a glance at Monica at his side, oddly confident and with a determined stride; Harjunpaa knew that had he been with Harko he might well have suggested they cut across the fields and take the safer route around.

They reached the top of the fields. Somebody was singing by the moose statue. Harjunpaa recalled that at least twice the police had found a man killed at the foot of this statue. Quite a crowd had gathered by the kiosk. Something was going on behind the bushes, near the pool. They could see something flailing, hear panting, then hoarse shouts followed by a burst of laughter. Monica touched Harjunpaa's hand. They stood still.

"Shall we skirt around?" Monica asked.

"We could go to the other side of those trees, the road's over there."

"OK."

They changed direction and walked hurriedly, without another word. Soon they could see over the bushes. A crowd of boys and girls stood at one end of the pool, all still very young, almost children. They formed a tight circle, electrified, sparking with excitement. There was panting, a stifled cry. Harjunpaa squatted. Between the legs of the crowd he could see jostling, the flash of a face, a bent arm—there were two of them, rolling on the ground, fighting fiercely but silently.

"Let's go!"

Harjunpaa rushed forward but Monica grabbed his sleeve.

46

"Timo! Don't be mad! We can't do anything on our own . . . there are dozens of them . . . they'll just turn on us . . . better get back to the car, radio for help."

Monica was already running toward the lane by the theater where their car was parked, hopelessly far away. Harjunpaa started after her, then hesitated. He knew Monica was right, but it would take at least five, maybe ten minutes before help would arrive. He looked at the crowd: The circle had broken. One of the fighters was up, the other still down, limbs convulsing as though in a fit. The one standing kicked the one on the ground, once, twice, three times. The kicks sounded oddly muffled, more like thumps.

"Monica," Harjunpaa shouted, pulling the car keys from his pocket and tossing them to her. "You go on . . . radio for help . . . say it's a policeman in trouble . . . I must do something or else we'll have another corpse on our hands."

Monica caught the keys, shouted something back angrily. Harjunpaa could not make out what it was. He was running toward the pool, and could see the teenagers now, and he was no longer afraid, only angry; being angry was dangerous. It made you incautious and liable to errors of judgment.

Harjunpaa rushed into the crowd at full speed, pushing his way to the front.

"Police!" he shouted. "That's enough!"

Both fighters were girls, the one on the ground screaming now, trying to cover her stomach with her hands. Her lips were bleeding. The face of the girl standing up was covered with scratches; her top was torn, half-pulled off, revealing a bare shoulder and a half-developed breast. She was aiming yet another kick when Harjunpaa grabbed her wrist and twisted her around. She shrieked and tried to steady her balance before falling.

"You idiots," Harjunpaa was panting now. He had a

47

notion there was something else he should do, but, could not remember what; everything had happened so quickly, he had had no time to plan anything. Out of the corner of his eye he could see the other girl crawling up, still clutching her stomach, and limping past the crowd.

The girl Harjunpaa had thrown on the ground was now back on her feet as well. She rushed at Harjunpaa, trying to scratch his face. He stepped back and grabbed her wrists again.

"What the hell do you want to interfere for!" she screamed, her face wet with sweat and sudden tears. "That's my sister and it's nobody's business if we fight."

"You might have killed her!"

"So what, I wanted to. She was snogging with my guy!"

The girl let out a howl and Harjunpaa released her wrists. She fell on her knees and covered her face.

Only now had Harjunpaa time to look around. They were all even younger than he had expected, either side of fifteen; there was something forbidding about them that made it difficult to think of them as children. These kids were not putting on an act because their parents weren't there; they probably had been on their own for years, done the rounds of reform schools. They might be just the ones he was looking for.

Harjunpaa was unsure. He was wondering whether Monica had reached the car and its radio yet.

The crowd was getting bigger—people had wandered over from the kiosk and from park benches, from the bushes and from further afield. There were now about thirty girls and boys. Harjunpaa was surrounded by a tight crowd, as the two fighters had been a few minutes earlier. Muscles around his eyes tightened but he thought he still had the initiative. He had to sham before they realized he was alone.

"Now start getting your ID cards out so we can see what sort of crowd you are." Harjunpaa was trying to show as much confidence as possible but his hands were shaking and sweat was trickling down his sides.

From the back of the crowd there were mutterings but nobody said anything until a voice behind his back shouted: "Start yourself. Start to scratch your arse."

Harjunpaa swerved around. The crowd was laughing, albeit cautiously as yet. Another voice shouted, "Hello, hello, hello, who's this then?"

"Look, it's a real pig. Piggy, piggy, piggy."

"Why aren't you flashing? The little pig can't flash!"

"It's not bright enough!"

Harjunpaa was breathing fast. The wall of jeans covered in felt-tip graffiti, of sleeveless shirts, of faces blurred with drink, was closing on him. There was no way he could break through. The butt of his revolver pressed between his arm and his hip, hard and angular. Harjunpaa knew it would be sheer madness to pull the revolver out now, since nothing really serious had happened yet. There were dozens of skirmishes like this every night. And besides, if he took his gun out now he could easily lose it—and then he would really be in trouble. He concentrated on the thought that right now Monica might be taking the microphone from its holder, or at least pushing the car key into the lock.

"Right. It's time you lot cleared off. Go! On your way." His voice was croaky as he turned round, as if to saunter away. But nobody made way for him.

"Man, you're treading on my foot!"

"Hey, the pig kicked Sepe!"

"Shut up!"

"Shut up yourself, pig, or we'll stuff your snout."

Harjunpaa said no more. He knew whatever he said would only make the situation worse. His fear grew, like a girdle, slowly pulled tighter. The foot on which he was resting his weight was shaking, almost out of control. A name echoed in his mind: "Taisto Nilsson. Taisto Nilsson. . . ." Now he knew what Nilsson must have experienced on Friday night—but he refused to think about what had followed once Nilsson was knocked down. He needed all his concentration to control the panic that was about to overwhelm him.

The crowd pressed closer, heaving restlessly. The air was thick with whispers and verbal assaults; a girl let out a shrill giggle. Somebody spat on Harjunpaa's shoes. A small pebble bounced off his shoulder. He attempted to look round and was met with a roar of laughter. A sickly smell of boozy breath surrounded his head.

"Shall we give the pig a swim?"

"No, we'll see if it's got any balls!"

"Bloody hell."

Harjunpaa felt a hard push on his shoulders. He took a quick step and was shoved in the chest. His hand moved down toward the holster; he had decided to shoot in the air. Somebody grabbed him by the collar and pulled. He was waving his arms around, helplessly.

"Pull his trousers down!"

"Let go! All of you! Don't move! Let go!"

The shout came from beyond the crowd. It was piercing, cutting through other noises like a knife. The laughter stopped abruptly, the grabbing hands held off. The gravel was crunching, sand flying, under running feet.

"This is the police!"

Only now Harjunpaa recognized Monica's voice. Suddenly there was space around him and he could see her about eleven yards away, standing between two tree trunks: legs apart, knees bent, arms extended. A gun was pointing toward the crowd.

"If you make one wrong move, any of you, you'll have nothing to hang between your legs tomorrow! Timo!"

Harjunpaa didn't lose a moment. He pushed his way through the remnants of the crowd and ran. Monica turned and headed away. Harjunpaa looked back. There was no longer anybody near the pool, only running shadows between the bushes, not one of them coming his way. Soon they were in Theater Lane and the sound of their running steps echoed from wall to wall. Railway Square was straight ahead, glowing with blue and orange light, full of cars and noise and people. To Harjunpaa it felt as if the real world was rushing toward him as he ran.

7

Harjunpaa sank to the front seat of the Lada, leaned his head on the neck rest, and panted. Sweat was pouring down his face, his shirt was soaked with it, sticking to his back. His hot mouth seemed to have grown too small to let enough air pass through to his demanding lungs.

"Damn, damn, damn."

"We must get them." Monica, too, was panting. "They're just the type of kids we're after here."

She was very pale, at some stage she had wiped her mouth so that lipstick made a line across her cheek. Her fingers were trembling as if she had just released some heavy burden, and she had to hold the microphone with both hands.

"Can Harko and Wallender hear on a direct line? This is Nisonen calling."

The reply was muffled and fragmented, ". . . you but . . . already in the garage . . . in Pasila . . . way out. . . ."

"They've finished already." Harjunpaa was trying to get his breath back, and ran his tongue over dry lips.

"Shall we try to get help from somewhere else?"

Harjunpaa thought about it. For some reason he believed that only two—at most three—people had been involved in beating Nilsson up. If that crowd, or that many, had been there, one or two of them would have remained sane and stopped the others before things got completely out of hand.

"No point." He still hadn't got his breathing steady.

"It's too late by now. They've all gone, vanished, every one of them. And besides, nothing really happened. Two girls were fighting, they wouldn't testify against each other, they were sisters. Better do it tomorrow, we'll have the whole place surrounded and get all their names and addresses."

Harjunpaa pressed his head against the wheel: It was hard and cold, reassuringly solid. He could feel his body gradually relaxing, but his legs still felt ready to run. Then they slowly became heavy, lifeless. His emotions were undergoing change as well—the fright, and the embarrassment that had followed, were now becoming mere memories.

He sat up and silently took Monica's hand. It was hot and her pulse fast, like a little bird's. He looked out of the window.

"Thanks a lot, Monica," he said in a hoarse voice. "I must have been mad. I believe . . . what you said about shooting their balls off did it. Had you said anything else they would have laughed at you."

"I thought . . . I was afraid . . . I thought I'd burst out crying any minute. If they hadn't believed me I would've cried, there was nothing else I could . . ."

She slid her hand free and looked for her cigarettes.

"I came after you almost at once," she said quietly. "I realized I'd never make it to the car, let alone get help there in time."

Harjunpaa remained silent. He switched the engine on. The clock in the station tower read ten to twelve. Somewhere in the far distance sirens were whining.

". . . coming over the bridge and approaching Pohjoisranta." They could hear the central duty officer booming through on the car radio. "A taxi is giving chase. We need a car on the other side to meet up. Anybody near enough?"

A short silence, then:

53

"1-2-2 in Tehtaankatu. Shall we try?"

"You're too far. Nobody closer by?"

"Some drunken driver," whispered Harjunpaa and engaged a gear.

". . . down Liisankatu and approaching Kaisaniemi Park. No cars at the station?"

Harjunpaa could feel Monica's look, but still he averted his own, didn't say anything. Tiredness had settled into an ache behind his eyes. His feet felt heavy and clumsy—he wanted no part in anything now, only to report back and catch a train home as soon as possible.

"Timo?"

"We'll wait. There are usually at least half a dozen cars near the station. . . ."

Harjunpaa slightly resented the eagerness to chase a car some of the police showed—all that fast driving with the sirens on, lights flashing, and no lengthy paperwork afterward. But let there be a report of a man lying in the street, dead, and all that followed was a deadly silence on the airwaves, broken finally by someone, halfheartedly.

"We have a definite registration number now," the radio announced. "It is U-L-H 8-8, white Ford Anglia . . . we had a report an hour ago the same car was stolen in Kontula. Are there no cars at the station?"

Harjunpaa nodded. Monica pressed the button.

"Central, 8-2-5 is near Station Square. We can take it!"

"You're right on the spot. 8-2-5 is on. Can 6-4-4 hear me? If you're still chasing, a car is now waiting at the station."

They could hear the sirens more clearly by now. Harjunpaa accelerated, changed gear. He didn't even try to go up and block the narrow street that led down to the square, there wasn't enough time for that. Instead he raced the car toward the station, aiming at the junction further on.

"Flash!" he yelled. "Get it up quickly!"

Monica bent down and searched round her feet. She jerked the flash from its holder, opened the window, and shoved the flash up on the roof, sorting out the cables with her other hand. Night air flooded in through the open window. Harjunpaa looked to his left and saw a white car, without lights, tilting as it turned the corner from the narrow street down toward the square. There was no sign of the police car. Harjunpaa put his foot down: He knew he could make it.

He brought the car to a stop with screeching breaks and squealing tires. The Lada was now in the middle of the junction. Harjunpaa fumbled under the dashboard, his fingers hit the cigarette lighter—now, here was the flash switch. He could hear through the car roof how the flash started to rotate, smearing everything around the Lada with blue light. Some people had stopped on the pavement, their faces staring, pale blotches. Suddenly he was nervous.

"What the hell!"

The Anglia was coming straight on. It was very near. Acceleration forced its nose up. It was like a giant frog, preparing to leap. Monica shouted. Harjunpaa let go of the wheel and threw himself to her side of the car. One word hammered in his head: Out! Out!

Next moment a white flash passed in front of the Lada, bounced over the pavement, and hit the tramlines, speeding away on the tracks.

"Damn it!"

Harjunpaa gritted his teeth so hard it hurt. He released the clutch and put his foot down hard on the accelerator. The Lada bounded forward. He turned the steering wheel violently, reached the tramlines, and changed gear. Monica switched on the siren; the tall buildings echoed and multiplied its anxious, urgent wail.

"Central, he got past . . . on the tramlines!" Monica was shouting into the microphone. "We're chasing him, we're right behind. Just coming up to Sokos corner . . . he's turning to go north on Mannerheimintie!"

"6-3-9 is by Finlandia House, we can take it from here."

"Central over and out."

Harjunpaa was breathing through his mouth. He preferred not to drive with the siren on; whenever possible; its monotonous wailing mesmerized him and made him lose all sense of speed.

"Take it easy," he told himself. "Take it easy." His feet were like two large, cumbersome animals, slow to respond to his commands. Just as well it was night, the streets empty. Now he could see blue flashes behind; the car that had first given chase was catching up with them.

"Two men in there," Monica shouted in his ear. "The one driving is tall. The other one is so short his head hardly shows over the back."

Two blue spots came alive outside Parliament House. They stood still for a second, then flashed through the night. The driver of the Anglia spotted them too, turned sharp right, the car swerved, straightened up, and sped down the sliproad.

"It's going down!" Monica shouted into the microphone.

"It hasn't got a chance! We'll block the way!" came the anonymous reply from the waiting car.

The Post house whizzed past, then the Rider statue. They lurched down the sliproad toward the freight depot. The waiting police car was blocking the other end, leaving too little space on either side for the Anglia to get past. Men were getting out already, running from the car. Harjunpaa had time to notice that one of them was flashing a red lamp.

The Anglia's brake lights came on, its nose dipped down. It slid to the right and stopped barely a yard from the wire fence that surrounded the freight depot. Both

56

doors burst open. Two men jumped out, one tall, the other very short. They ran to the fence, jumped up, and started to climb over.

Harjunpaa came to a halt next to the Anglia.

"The car has been caught by the freight depot," Monica was reporting. "There are two of them, trying to get over the fence to the warehouses. We're following." Harjunpaa was already out of the car, striding toward the fence, one hand pushing his jacket aside, reaching for his gun. The taller man was on the top of the fence, was throwing one leg over. "Halt!" Harjunpaa shouted. There was a dark streak on the other side, followed by a thump, then the man was bent low, running across the tracks toward the warehouses.

The other man—or rather youth—hadn't got halfway up the fence. He hung on the wire desperately, kicking out with his feet. Harjunpaa reached for one leg.

"OK, mate, no need to thrash so."

The boy let go and slid down. Harjunpaa put his hand on his shoulder; he could feel the boy trembling, almost shaking, as if it was midwinter and really cold. He had a child's face. He looked at the gun in Harjunpaa's hand with wide eyes, folding both arms slowly across his chest. Harjunpaa pushed his gun back in its holster.

"Shall we chase?" Monica asked. She swept the darkness on the other side of the fence with her searchlight. On the ground, where the other boy had landed, was a peaked cap, black and without a badge.

"No point without the dogs," Harjunpaa said.

The police Saab rolled down to the other side of the Anglia. One of the patrolmen was talking into the microphone—Harjunpaa thought he was asking for dogs. The Saab's flash had been switched off but the Lada was still standing there, both doors wide open, engine on, light flashing on its roof, and the siren still wailing.

8

Harjunpaa lit a cigarette and dragged on it so hard a tarry line appeared on the filter. He was standing at the doorway of the interview room, trying to blow the smoke out into the corridor.

The boy was sitting on a bench that was steel-bolted to the concrete floor. He looked barely fifteen. Standing up he measured a meager 5 feet 3 inches; when sitting hunched up, like now, he was a pitifully small bundle. His denim jacket had no sleeves and the arms sticking out of the black T-shirt were so slender they seemed almost shriveled. His hands, too, were small and soft-looking, with nails bitten to the quick.

So far he had said nothing—not even his name, nothing.

"Do you feel like talking now?" Harjunpaa tried once more, although he might just as well have left the whole matter to the uniform branch. "I'm not threatening you, I'm simply telling you how things stand: Sooner or later you've got to talk. You won't get out of it like this. You must realize that."

The boy's lips trembled, then he muttered in a tight voice, "Beat me up. You can beat me up as much as you want."

Harjunpaa caught his eye and the boy tried to stare back with blue eyes too full of anxiety for his age—and somehow you could tell that the bravado was only on the surface; deep inside he wanted to give in. Harjunpaa said nothing.

The boy started to blink—slowly at first, then very rapidly, and when the tears came he bent down and covered his head, as if to protect himself. Harjunpaa sighed. He knew he had won but the victory gave him no pleasure. What he felt was something akin to shame, mixed with pity and aimless anger or frustration. He walked tiredly into the room and sat down next to the boy, who instantly drew away.

"Take it easy, man. This isn't the end of the world."

He waited until the worst sobbing was over. Then he asked, "Well, what's your name?"

"Mikael. Mikael Bergman."

"And how old are you?"

"Fourteen."

And who was the other one, the one driving the Anglia?"

Mikael was silent. Harjunpaa could sense how he tensed and hesitated. Somehow Harjunpaa knew it wasn't just the ordinary loyalty of not snitching on a mate—he was sure Mikael hadn't been caught before, he wasn't hardened—no, there was something else in it, some odd fear, but he simply didn't have the energy to start to dig around the finer points.

"Well, who was it?"

"I don't . . . I think it . . ."

"Didn't you hear what Harjunpaa asked?"

Tillander from the vehicle department bustled in: a short man always in a rush. He threw the plastic bag that contained Mikael's few possessions on the table and flipped the peaked cap onto the boy's head, shaking it by the eye shade. The cap was far too big, falling over Mikael's ears.

"Not yours," Tillander commented. "Your head's not thick enough. That's why you got caught. Well, who was that thick-headed mate of yours?"

"I don't know. I thumbed a lift and . . ."

Tillander laughed a long throaty laugh.

"Wasn't that just your luck! You know, you must be the millionth person caught in a stolen car who was just a hitchhiker! Never mind, we'll celebrate your lift. We'll invite your mum and dad to call. Parents are always so delighted when they get an invitation in the middle of the night to come and collect their little hitchhikers. And then the four of us can have a little chat and then you might just remember that the driver did introduce himself when he gave you a lift. Timo . . ."

Tillander drew Harjunpaa out of the room.

"Can you take him upstairs, to some waiting room, and keep an eye on him for a while. I've been so hellishly busy all night. I've got two men locked up, waiting for me to come and say hello . . . in a way you owe this one to me—the whole show should have gone over to the eastern district, that's where the car was stolen. I need to take a quick look at the car, too. Check the wires and so on. I'll ring his home. Will you keep an eye?"

Harjunpaa's face was devoid of any expression, his eyes so narrow they were almost shut. Had Harko been there he might have known how to read that face. He looked at his watch, just gone half past twelve. The next—and last—train would leave in an hour; he had an hour to spare.

"OK. But at twenty past one I'm going, regardless of how many men you have lined up waiting to say hello."

"Come on, come on, Timo. . . . Hey, sonny, what's your phone number?"

"This way," said Harjunpaa. He sensed a change in Mikael but they were in the elevator before he realized what it was: The boy was no longer tense. He wasn't relaxed in the way a suspect might be when he feels his case is settled—instead he was dozy, almost apathetic, as killers sometimes were. Harjunpaa was mildly amused; after all, it was only a car, a pile of tin and rubber and iron, never mind that some poor sod had sweated and saved to become its happy owner.

The elevator stopped and the doors opened.

"Here we go."

Mikael didn't move. He leaned against the wall and stared at the buttons on the wall as if he were asleep with his eyes wide open.

"Well?"

"I'll die for this," Mikael said quietly. "My dad'll kill me."

Harjunpaa cleared his throat. He was about to say "Come off it" when he took a closer look at Mikael's face and couldn't say anything at all. He had the same uneasy feeling as when reading something dreadful in his morning paper. He tried to comfort himself by thinking that appearances are deceptive, that the boy was exaggerating, but the unease wouldn't go away. He took Mikael to the same waiting room where—a small eternity ago—a man had asked him to touch a bulging vein.

Then he went to the control room.

"That patrol car took Monica home," said the duty officer. "What . . ." but before he could get any further Tillander rushed in.

"A bloody good thing we brought him upstairs," he said eagerly. "You know what, that kid's dad is in the force!"

The duty officer looked at Tillander over his spectacles.

"You mean he's a policeman's son?"

"Indeed. His father is a constable in 1K."

Harjunpaa got the distinct feeling that there was as much malice as there was surprise in Tillander's voice.

"On the other hand," Tillander went on, "quite a few in the force have kids that have gone rotten. Paulin—his oldest daughter is on drugs and is picked up pretty often.

And both of Holm's sons take it in turns to be caught thieving. Now why the hell should that be?"

"Maybe it's an occupational hazard," Harjunpaa said quietly, thinking of Pauliina and Valpuri, and how little time he had to spend at home, and how he felt half-dead inside, and how he was often irritable, and how his daughters then looked at him, silently.

"An occupational hazard?" Tillander looked baffled. Then he laughed, as he had a little earlier downstairs in the interview room. "You mean daddy brings home some criminal bugs on his uniform? What will you dream up next! An occupational hazard to have rotten kids. . . . By the way, his parents are on their way. His mother insisted she come as well. I'll have a few words with that lad, get something on paper. You tell me when they're here."

Harjunpaa glanced at his watch; another half an hour to go. He clambered over the reception desk and joined the duty officer.

Ten minutes later car lights swept across the entrance. The duty officer pressed a button and the monitor beneath his desk showed a large, shining Volvo—a woman wearing a headscarf was locking the door on the driver's side; a fat man opened the passenger door. He seemed to be talking angrily.

A moment later they were in the entrance hall. The man was in his early fifties, with a large belly. The woman looked younger, and kept well behind her husband. The duty officer whispered to Harjunpaa, "The most difficult people are well-educated women who have had too much to drink. Next come policemen whose kids have got into trouble."

The man opened the door to the duty officer's room. The woman stayed in the hall. Harjunpaa thought she might have been crying—she looked down, her scarf was covering part of her face, and she toyed with her car keys nervously.

62

"Bergman," the man announced. "Our son is here, somebody called Tillander rang."

Harjunpaa hadn't recognized Bergman before, the clothes were different. Out there, by the bay, Bergman had been wearing a uniform; now he was dressed in a khaki shirt, armpits black with sweat, and a cap, like a baseball cap, with rows of badges around the sides. Harjunpaa didn't think Bergman recognized him. Bergman leaned his thick strong arms on the desk—now that he was closer Harjunpaa could see the beads of sweat on his forehead. His breathing was noisy and he sucked on some strong-smelling sweet; it almost covered the smell of alcohol on his breath.

Tillander was hurrying down the corridor, his beeper buzzing in his pocket.

The duty officer put the receiver down and introduced, "The Bergmans."

"This way, this is where we're keeping your black sheep." Tillander was trying to sound jovial and understanding. Bergman followed him; his wife remained in the hall.

"He was nearly normal," said Harjunpaa.

"Well." The duty officer put both hands behind his head and leaned as far back as the chair would allow. "We were on the same training course. He was somewhat peculiar already by then. Now it's clear he's got some nuts loose somewhere. There was some trouble with his older boy. He died couple of years back—rode a stolen motorbike, together with some other kid, straight into traffic lights. . . . I've got a sister-in-law, works in the same hospital as Bergman's wife. From what I gather from what she's been saying, Bergman won't even visit the kid's grave—because it was a stolen bike."

"Bloody hell."

"Yep. You know, he used to work here in the early sixties. In embezzlement. But then his first wife was killed.

63

Shot—or shot herself. And with his service gun, too. Vilkman was still in charge of violent crimes then and he had Bergman arrested. Spent three days in the nick, never said a word. Then they got a witness and had to let Bergman go. In the end it was filed as suicide. But ever since he's been a bit bitter toward us in here."

They sat still for a few minutes. Mrs. Bergman paced up and down in the hall; she would stop, stare at something, and then pace again. She moved restlessly and aimlessly, like a caged animal, looking up from time to time, as if expecting to hear something.

"I must catch my train." There was still plenty of time, but Harjunpaa hoped he'd feel better outside—the heaviness in his head was still there and he feared it might turn into a migraine.

Harjunpaa walked round the reception desk and out into the hall. He had reached the door before he realized Mrs. Bergman had followed him. When he stopped she stayed a few yards away, looked into his face briefly, then looked down again. She seemed surprisingly young, barely forty—but there was a worn look on her face and the hasty makeup gave her a forlorn appearance.

"Could you," she began, then thought better of it and stopped. She swallowed so hard he could see the muscles move in her neck. "Would you be so kind and tell his father that he . . ."

"Yes?"

"Forget it. Sorry. . . ."

She turned and almost ran back to the hall. Harjunpaa didn't leave immediately. He couldn't marshal his thoughts. In the end he decided that Mrs. Bergman had probably only wanted assurance that the matter would go no further.

Harjunpaa pushed the door open and stepped out into the night. He knew it would be hours before he would get any sleep.

9

Mikael eased his grip on the balcony railing. For a brief moment he was hanging in the air before managing to grasp a branch of the birch tree—but not securely enough to stop the fall; on his way down the twigs tore at his face, his neck, his body.

Then he hit the ground.

He keeled over and could feel the grass and soil under his hands.

Mikael forced himself to move before his father could find him, only to stumble over a bench and fall down again. Lights came on in the living room, throwing a pale yellow glow over the lawn. Mikael crashed through a flowerbed, reached the hedge—again he was caught in tearing branches and had to force his way through. On the other side of the hedge he jumped over the ditch and scrambled into the field.

Only when he had reached the playing field did he dare to look back.

His mother was sitting in the living room. She was in an armchair, holding her head in her hands, rocking herself from side to side. There was no sign of Sod. He might still be in his own room. No—Mikael could hear him shouting now, he was hoarse with rage.

"Mikael!"

The voice came through the balcony door. He should have closed it, only there had been no time. Grabbing him by the scruff of his neck, Sod had marched him in from the car, pushed him up the stairs and through the door to his room. He had not said a word, but his breathing had been hard and fast. After locking Mikael in he had taken his bunch of keys and gone to his small room downstairs. Mikael had not waited to see what would happen next. He had rushed to the balcony and away.

"Mikael!"

The voice was louder, he must be on the balcony now.

Mikael sprinted away across the field. On one side were two sheds, he could see them as two dark splotches, darker than the background. Mikael headed toward the sheds and crawled into the black gap between them. He crouched in the darkness, panting and sweating.

Thoughts bounced wildly round his head.

He had no money, not a penny, and he had nowhere to go. He could never return home, never. Sod would surely kill him. Even here he could stay only for a moment, he had to press on. Once, last winter, when someone had broken the car aerial, Sod had taken his police truncheon and stayed out half the night looking for the culprits. He had never said whether he had found them, but the following night the rubbish-bin shed had burned down and two cars had burned as well.

"Miku."

Mikael scrambled up and pressed himself against the wall. Then he realized it was Leo's voice. "Leo . . . Sid!"

"I'm here, wait a sec, I'll come down. I saw you running."

Leo was on the roof of the bigger shed. It was a good place to be. Mikael had often been there himself: Up there you could feel you had escaped everything, nobody was breathing down your neck. Lying up there, on your back, arms behind your head, you could see all the countless stars, like small holes puncturing the sky. The tarred felt roof rustled as Leo skidded down. His legs appeared above the drainpipe and in one leap he stood next to

Mikael. At once Mikael felt much better. It was the same feeling you got when you were out on your own and saw a strange gang coming, and just when you were getting really scared, one of them recognized you and said, "Hi, Miku!" and it was all right.

"You should've seen how I ran," Leo was babbling. He smelled of booze and was oddly excited. "I ran across the whole bloody rail yard. I thought I would spit my lungs out, I ran that hard. I knew they would bring dogs there, they always do when they lose someone. I ran all the way to the station and then I just got on a platform and walked out. I hope the dogs went that way and that some hot-dog man got his arse bitten!"

Leo honked with laughter, almost hysterical.

"They got your cap," Mikael said. The laughter stopped. Leo went rigid, then flinched, as if hurt—or as if punching someone there in the dark.

"Those bastards, so they did. . . . My cap."

Leo sounded strange; Mikael had never heard him like that. If it had been someone else it would have sounded almost like crying. Mikael had to look away, even in the dark.

"They've got my cap in their filthy hands," Leo said wretchedly. "Trying it on their greasy pig heads. My cap! You don't understand. I've got to have it! When I have that cap on I can take any shit coming. I don't care one fuck how happy or rich other people think they are, I have my cap. . . . And when I pull it right down, I can peer out at those shits, and no one dares say anything to me. It doesn't matter what I am or who . . . when I've got my cap they're all afraid."

"But they've got it."

"I know. Bastards."

Mikael wished he hadn't mentioned the cap. He did not want Leo to cry—the whole idea was so horrible that it could only bring about other horrible things.

"Let's get out of here," he said. "Sod is after me. I think he went to get a torch and his truncheon. He's probably on his way right now."

"Why don't we beat him up? He's always been against me . . . when Jani and me were mates he was always on about me to Jani. He told Jani not to hang around with me . . . he called me a rat and said my mum is a whore . . . well, she is, a real prickhole at that, but why don't we beat him up? I feel like beating someone up, you know, really bad. Since they got my cap."

Mikael stared at Leo, mesmerized. Something was welling up inside. He could imagine Sod lying on the ground—all the buttons from his shirt torn off, his huge, flabby belly exposed. His fat lips were covered in sand, he was trying to spit it out as he scrambled to get up. But he couldn't make it, he fell back under the force of their kicks, their boots smacking into his fat. Mikael felt his cheeks burn as he said stiffly: "That would serve that shitbelly right."

"He's bigger than us. If we can knock him down it's his own fault."

"Bloody hell."

The boys crouched and peered around the corner of the shed. In the field nobody was moving; there were no sounds. The light was still on in Mikael's living room.

"Maybe he won't come."

"He's sure to. He was hopping mad. He was so mad his face was scarlet and all the veins were popping up."

A car drove past the houses. Somewhere further away a dog barked. And then a light from a torch flashed on the grass near the house.

"He's coming," Mikael whispered. His heart beat wildly and his fingers seemed to want to grab at something. His father was pointing the torch on the flowerbeds and the ditch—now he was pushing his way through the hedge. Leo made eager little grunts.

"I've got something," he said, groping under the shed. He pulled out a yard-long piece of timber with two large nails sticking out at one end.

"This will fell him in one swoop."

Sod was making his way across the field. He waved the torch about; the beam was like a walking lighthouse. They could hear his footsteps. Leo squeezed Mikael's shoulder.

"We'll let him get between the two sheds," Leo whispered in a shaky voice. "We'll hide behind and when he comes round the corner, we'll . . ." The boys stood up in readiness.

Still some sixty yards away, Sod stopped. He switched the torch off and dissolved into the darkness. Fear grabbed Mikael's belly. Suddenly Sod could be anywhere, even standing right behind them.

"Leo, let's scram."

"No!"

Mikael peeped around the corner again. Sod had lit a cigarette; Mikael could see the red, glowing dot. Now it disappeared, glowed again, further down—Sod was going back, smoking as he went. Mikael felt weak at the knees.

"Shit!" You could tell by Leo's voice that he was gritting his teeth.

"I bet he's going to beat your mum up."

"Yeah."

"Best be off. He might get it into his head to take the car and go snooping around the shopping center. Or else get some other bright ideas."

The boys crossed the corner of the playing field and pushed through some bushes to get to the footpath.

"They made me say it was you who was driving." Mikael felt awkward and did not dare look at Leo.

"Oh really? Well, I should have guessed."

Leo was quiet for a long time. He had not sounded

69

angry but scornful and Mikael felt he had to justify himself. "They had me in a white room and kept asking, again, and again . . . at least a million times. Sod was there as well. But I didn't say a word. But then Sod said to the other policeman that if he'd split for a while Sod could clear the matter up in a minute. The other pig said at first that he couldn't do it. Then he laughed and said he'd pop to the loo. He got to the door . . . and I had to tell them . . . but you sure were some driver . . . you were going like hell."

"Yeah?" Leo chuckled. "Wasn't I just? That was a tight corner when the police Lada cut in front of us. It was like the whole world was one flashing blue light. At first I thought I'd rip straight in and have one almighty smash to end it all . . . but then I saw the tramlines."

"You dropped your cap by the fence."

"I didn't know it had gone till I stopped running. But I'll get it back. And your dad will be beaten up. I'll give him such a beating that he'll beg me to let him fetch my cap back from the cops."

The boys came to a halt near Leo's house. Most of the windows were dark. When you stared at the dark windows you felt very clearly that there were homes in the building, that people were sleeping in there, and had no idea that someone was standing outside with nowhere to go. Mikael felt very empty. He almost thought it was a pity he had not been shot by the fence.

"What're we going to do?" he asked in a small voice.

"I could do with some booze. If I got some booze I might sleep a little. Or if I got a lot of booze I could go and liven things up a bit."

"I shan't ever be able to go home again."

"We can go to my house. We can kick my mother out. That would be only fair, she's kicked me out often enough. Or else you could sleep on the sofa."

"No." Mikael was adamant. The mere thought of get-

70

ting any closer to the house scared him. He was sure that Sod had driven over and was now waiting in the shadows. "They know you were driving, they might be waiting inside for you to turn up. Or else they'll come in the morning. That's how they always do it. Dad told me once that morning is the best time to make arrests because people are so dozy they never know what's happened until they're sitting in the police car on the way to the nick."

"It was morning when they took me in."

The boys were standing still. Helplessness was like some sticky substance. Once it got hold of you it couldn't be shaken off. A sound of breaking glass came from the shopping center.

"Oh, fuck it," Leo said finally. "Why don't we go to my tent in the cave. I've been there at night before. It's a bit chilly, damp, you know, but we can take some blankets along. Hey, I know! We can take food and some booze and have a fire in the cave. We can get the stuff from home . . . we can go in sort of quietly and find out if anybody is waiting for us before we step into it. Come on."

Mikael chewed his fingernails. There was something horrible about the cave—it was so very still and yet so full of sounds—but the thought of the fire cheered him up. He could almost see the sausages sizzling and the flames reflecting on the water.

"OK." He sighed his acquiescence.

There was nobody near the house. And there were no Ladas about, equipped with two wing mirrors and a short, stubby aerial. The boys slipped up the staircase in the dark, to the fifth floor. It was so quiet they could hear Leo's watch.

Both boys were panting slightly by the time they got there.

"Hold on a tick."

Leo knelt down in front of the door. He pushed his

71

fingers through the letter box, which hung loose in its fittings. It had been pulled out once too often and nobody had taken the trouble to fasten it back securely. When you pulled the flap and the frame off you could slip your hand in and unlock the door. Leo stood up. In the dim light from the staircase windows Mikael saw that his face had gone hard.

"My mum's in," he said in a low voice. "And she's got some man in there, too. They're fucking."

"Better not go in."

"Shit! Who cares."

Leo took his key and opened the door. The boys stepped in. Mikael held his breath. The smell of Leo's home was foul, maybe it came from dirty clothes strewn all over the place, or from something gone sour, or from fungus growing under the lino. A streak of light came from the sitting room. By the bathroom door, against the opposite wall, were three overflowing bags of rubbish; a tin of pickled herring had rolled onto the mat from one of the bags. The boys could hear Leo's mother in the next room. She was saying in a coaxing voice: "Come on, why don't you give it another try?" A hoarse drunken voice answered something indistinct.

Mikael felt sick. He leaned on the wall and closed his eyes. For a moment he was still hanging on the wire fence; then the stench of pickled herring penetrated his consciousness again and he felt he had to get away, not to say anything to Leo, just slip out and go to Ulla's place. Ulla would let him into her bed and would hold him tight.

"Miku, get a blanket from my bed. I'll get something to eat and if those two have any booze I'll take that as well. And if she tries any mouthing off you don't take any notice."

"Look, better not go in. I think I'll just . . ."

But Leo didn't listen. He pushed the door wide open

72

and marched in. Mikael hung back, by the door. The air in the room was even stuffier, like the gym dressing room at school. Mikael was embarrassed, yet couldn't help looking. They were both on the bed, both were naked. Leo's mother was all pale flesh; she had huge tits, both clearly visible. The man had hidden his face in the pillows, but he hadn't removed his hand from her crotch.

Leo's mum lifted her head. She looked befuddled, unaware of anything around her. Her eyes reminded Mikael of Sod's eyes when he was about to drop off.

"Is that you, Leo?"

"Shit!"

Leo went straight to the kitchen and banged cabinet doors.

"Leo, you shouldn't bring people in in the middle of the night."

"And what about you? Or is that a member of the family you have there in bed with you?"

Leo was banging around in the kitchen. You could hear him wrapping something in paper and stuffing it into a plastic bag. Mikael felt even more embarrassed, for Leo's sake, for having a mother like that.

"Oh, good grief," she said in a limp voice. The man was snoring gently.

The floor was strewn with clothes and empty beer bottles. The table was covered with all sorts of stuff, overflowing ashtrays, wine bottles, glasses. Leo came back with a bulging plastic bag. On his way through he picked up two full bottles and a packet of cigarettes and stuffed them in.

"You leave those alone, son."

Leo's mother was sitting up. She held a sheet up to her chin in a bout of belated modesty. Her head was nodding from side to side. Leo stopped by the bed and took hold of the blanket on which she was sitting, and tugged furiously. She keeled over. Then Leo yanked off a second blanket, rumpled up behind the man.

73

"That's enough, Leo!"

"Yeah, enough for me," Leo answered. "You keep fucking, then you won't feel the cold. See ya!"

On his way out Leo stepped on the man's trousers and dragged them with his feet out of the room. Once in the hall he bent down and swiftly removed the wallet from the back pocket. There were a couple of big notes and a few smaller ones, all of which Leo took. He shoved the wallet back into the pocket and threw the trousers back into the room. He grinned, trying to smile, but his lips trembled so you couldn't look at him, and then his eyes became shiny.

"Bloody hell," he said through gritted teeth, in the same way he had spoken about his cap. "Sometimes I would just like to take a knife to them and pin both to the bed!"

"Leo . . . Sid!"

"Bloody hell! Shall I?"

"Let's go, Sid. Let's get out of here."

Mikael took the blankets. Leo kicked the door shut so hard that the echo in the stairwell sounded like a shot.

Leo's mother sat up.

Her first name was Kaarina, her surname Melin. She was forty-five years old. She had been a machinist in a clothing factory but had been out of work for the past eighteen months—and she wasn't sure if she minded that too much.

She was still officially married but had not seen her husband for four years. Somehow there had not seemed much point in getting a divorce—too much trouble, running around from one office to another, getting all sorts of papers together, no point in all that. Besides, her husband was in Sweden somewhere.

"Was that your son?" the man asked from behind her back.

"Yep. That was my son."

"You should've told me. I would've brought him something."

"Well, yes. My son. I tell you he would not be like that if I had had my way with him. But Johan, that's my husband, he thought he knew better . . . you see, his father was a fascist and he got beaten up all the time as a kid . . . he was always crying about it when he got drunk."

She reached for a glass on the table, half full, and drained the wine in one gulp.

"So Leo always got his way. I remember how once he kicked over—kicked, you know, didn't knock it over by accident—a bucket of water when I'd been washing the floors . . . did I want to get him by the short and curlies and tell him what I thought of him! But Johan told me to shut up. And then, after Johan left, he got worse and worse, now he's been kicking me around for years." She covered her face with her hands and blubbered. The man said nothing.

After a while she blew her nose and took a deep breath. She fished out half a cigarette from the ashtray, and got it going, inhaling deeply.

"But Johan had some crazy ideas at times. When Leo was ten, can you guess what Johan got him for his birthday? A bottle of vodka. But we drank it all by ourselves after Leo was sick with two sips. Are you listening? You asleep? Hey."

She shook the man by his bare flank but got no response.

"I should've guessed, asleep, of course."

She got carefully out of the bed and went to his trousers with an unsteady step. The wallet in the back pocket was empty. She dropped the trousers back on the floor and returned to the bed, stumped out her fag, and when she'd crawled in, started to nudge the man out of his sleep.

"Come on. Let's get going. One proper round at least."

10

Monica pushed the tap lever with her elbow, got the water running, and started to wash her hands. The smell of antiseptic spread through the room. Harjunpaa busied himself with his paper cap. His hair was too long at the back and wouldn't stay inside; it was the cap that had distracted him. Last time he had been required to wear one was five years ago: It had been night, in the maternity hospital where he had gone with Elisa to have Valpuri. They had put the baby in his arms, wrapped in paper, unwashed and tacky, and for some silly reason he had thought that the baby was smiling at him, at the cap on his head.

"Hands once more," said the nurse waiting at the door. Harjunpaa moved to the basin, stealing a sideways look at Monica. You wouldn't have recognized her but for her eyes; they were gray, like water, with a thin bluish ring around the iris. Like Harjunpaa, she was dressed in a long, green overall that flapped around her ankles; in the paper cap; a mask covering half her face; and in white socks over which white plastic slippers, almost like plastic bags, had been pulled.

"This way," the nurse called, and Monica and Harjunpaa followed her down the corridor.

Harjunpaa had telephoned the hospital first thing that morning. To his surprise he had been told that Nilsson had regained consciousness the day before and could even answer questions to some degree, mostly by nodding

76

or shaking his head. After some hesitation the doctor had given them permission to interview Nilsson—this was rare with someone in intensive care and Harjunpaa had guessed that the improvement was likely to be only temporary, that they were expecting things to go wrong. One of the first lessons he had learned when he had started to deal with victims of violence was that the rot set in easiest in the stomach, boosted by the patient's own bacteria.

The departmental head had agreed that Monica and Wallender could temporarily work with Norri. Ordinarily summertime was the busiest season for the section that dealt with vice and sex crimes, and Monica could not have been spared, but by a rare and lucky coincidence the section had a full complement of staff, five, at the moment. Wallender's section was not quite so lucky: Only one man remained there.

They stopped at a pair of green swing doors. Red letters across the door declared: NO ADMITTANCE INTENSIVE CARE. The nurse stepped aside and nodded. Harjunpaa pushed the doors open. There was yet another corridor and a new set of doors—these were half glass and Harjunpaa could see into the well-illuminated room: a desk with a nurse sitting at it. The sterile smell was even stronger here, but mixed with something else, reminiscent of wet metal or ozone. Harjunpaa fumbled with the cassette recorder he was carrying, and found himself nervous; in fact he felt almost as he had all those years back, during his first autopsy. Then he had thought he'd faint.

They went through the second pair of doors and the nurse came to meet them.

"You're from the police? Nisonen and Harjunpaa?" Harjunpaa nodded. All he could see of the nurse was her eyes. Somehow it was odd that she sounded so perfectly normal—you would have expected her to sound like a machine.

"Mr. Nilsson is over here."

They moved farther into the room. Another nurse appeared from somewhere and occupied the seat by the desk vacated by their guide. The light in the room wasn't harsh and it cast no shadows. Harjunpaa couldn't figure out how that was achieved. The room was full of strange, quiet sounds: hissing pumps, bubbling noises, bleeps, and a sound like a frozen sea melting in the spring sun. There was a quiet moan.

They stopped at a bed surrounded by mysterious equipment. Taisto Nilsson was lying on his back, naked. He was strapped to the bed by his wrists and ankles. His stomach was covered with bandages through which tubes protruded—Harjunpaa didn't even try to count how many. A pinkish liquid bubbled through the tubes to containers on the floor. Taisto's face was covered with surgical tape; underneath were black stitches like worms—his skin had a yellowish tinge, it looked like melted and rehardened plastic.

Harjunpaa lifted the recorder to his mouth: "This interview with Taisto Nilsson is taking place in the intensive care unit at the hospital." He spoke breathlessly; the mask made him feel he couldn't breathe properly and he tried furtively to detach it from his face. The nurse bent over the bed.

"Taisto, there are some people here to see you," she said. "Two of them, from the police. Do you think you could answer some questions?"

"Interviewer is Detective Inspector Timo Harjunpaa, witnessed by Detective Sergeant Monica Nisonen. Reference R-V-A-stroke-one-five-four-zero-two."

Harjunpaa felt like a kid at school, one who has forgotten well-memorized lines. He unfolded the sheet of paper, which stuck to his fingers.

Can you remember what happened and when?
Did you know the people who attacked you? How many
people were there?

78

How old were they? What size? What were they wearing?
Anything else you can tell me about their appearance?
How and where did you meet them?
Was there an argument about something?
How did they attack you?
Was anything taken from you?
What time was it?
Can you remember anything else?

Harjunpaa refolded the piece of paper. Seen like this the questions seemed childish—but they covered the key points and if they got an answer to even some of these they would have taken a giant leap forward.

The nurse was frowning. She glanced at the oscilloscope above the bed, at the green line bobbing on its screen, bent down to check one of the containers on the floor, touched one of the tubes, and ran her fingers quickly over Nilsson's belly.

"Just a minute." She walked quickly over to the desk and spoke into the intercom: "Kallio? Could you come at once. It's the stomach case." She bent down over the intercom and they lost the rest of her words. Monica looked at Harjunpaa. Harjunpaa pressed the recorder button and bent over the bed.

"Taisto. My name is Timo. Are you able to speak at all?" Nilsson moved, tossed his head restlessly as if trying to fight free of the straps. Then he made an effort to move his lips. They parted with difficulty. Harjunpaa bent closer still.

"Are you even human?" The words came through so quietly that they were barely audible.

11

Pasilan Lane was less than five miles north of the heart of Helsinki. It ran near the railway tracks that separated it from the TV studio complex.

So far the only building on the lane was Number 13, built for the police. From a distance the building looked like a shoebox, faded in the sunlight, but this box had three flagpoles and a radio mast on its roof. Nearby were some old, decrepit, timber houses, some building sites where drills screamed all day long, and a little further away some nearly completed, massive office buildings.

In the early planning stages there had been talk about making this into the headquarters for SUOPO. But then the emergency department and the dog handlers and the assistant chief constable moved in as well, and it was not called headquarters of anything, just police quarters. The only remnant of any detective spirit was maybe in the fact that on the approach to the building there were no signs to give any clues to its function. Only in the enclave above the main entrance—which faced the trees, not the lane—could one see a discreet, blue plastic sign with the word: POLICE.

Although the building appeared to be shaped like a shoebox it was actually triangular—a wing protruded from the western end. This wing had five floors. The topmost floor housed one of the specialist sections within SUOPO, fire and explosives, and one of the general sections that was led by Norri. Both sections could work uninterrupted by any casual visitors, for the elevators stopped at the fourth floor and so did the main staircase. The only means of reaching the fifth floor was by a narrow, spiral staircase.

Harjunpaa was now bounding up these winding stairs. He was in no particular hurry, it just was his habit. Monica came after him, heels clicking on the steps.

"What d'you think happened?" she panted.

"Didn't dare ask, they seemed to be in such a tearing rush. But I suspect they were going to operate again. The last nurse was asking the theater to stand by for an emergency."

They reached the corridor on the fifth floor. A typewriter was being tapped in a slow, ponderous manner somewhere, the intercom beeped behind a door nearby. Harjunpaa made straight for Norri's door and opened it without waiting for the green entry light.

"I'm so sorry."

Someone was in the room with Norri. Harjunpaa was about to close the door again when Norri gestured for him to wait.

"Timo, wait. Mrs. Asp, will you excuse me."

He nodded to the woman sitting opposite his desk and searched his drawer for a sheet of paper. Harjunpaa's eyes narrowed; he could tell something had turned up, otherwise Norri wouldn't have interrupted an interview. Harjunpaa recognized the woman now—her husband and thirteen-year-old son had clashed the previous week, the father holding a fishknife and the son wielding a heavy piece of copper piping. Now the son was in one hospital with a stab wound in his chest, his father in another with a broken jawbone and blind in one eye.

"Did you have any luck?" Norri asked after closing the door.

"No. He suddenly turned for the worse . . . I think

81

they're operating again. Monica and I were thrown out in our paper caps."

"Read this."

Norri handed him the sheet of paper. It was the daily report from Lost and Found. The ninth entry was underlined in red: "Ref 3541—man's watch, digital. Lambda Alarm Chronograph. With inscription: T.N. 31.10.80. Found on Lampipolku, Kontula."

Harjunpaa sucked his breath in; he could feel his blood run faster. He looked at Norri.

"The date of the inscription fits. It was a thirty-fifth birthday present from the mother."

"I've sent the men there," said Norri in a low voice. They're putting together a list of all incidents reported in Kontula that night. On their way back they'll pick up the watch from Lost and Found; we'll have it checked for any prints. We can go over everything in detail once I'm through with this interview."

Harjunpaa and Monica looked at each other—both knew that the watch might lead somewhere. But there was another possibility: The assailants might have sold the watch at the station on the night of the attack.

They went to Harjunpaa's office. From the window they could see Helsinki—Harjunpaa had once counted at least seven church towers, the cathedral most prominent. In the old offices, near the cathedral, he had time and time again seen how sunset colored its west side orange and sunrise made the east side pink. Harjunpaa sat on the edge of his desk.

"Where do we start?"

"Hold on."

Thoughts were tumbling in his head. He was trying to sort them out, make sure that nothing was forgotten. All reports for Kontula for the night in question had to be sifted again; they'd have to consult the section that dealt with robberies, and with the police in charge of the eastern part of Helsinki—including Kontula. There might be something in this case that reminded someone there of some other incident; they'd have to check back for a couple of years and see if something like this had happened in Kontula before—and he'd have to remember to ring home and let them know he might be late again. Last night when he had got home and helped Valpuri on her potty, she had said, half-asleep: "Daddy will you run away again in the morning?"

"Monica, why don't we split it up so that you go through the—"

"Morning."

Tornberg had appeared at the door. He was a temporary holiday relief, a quiet man who didn't waste words. Sometimes—more often than not—he'd look away and laugh to himself after taking in what the others had been saying or doing.

"Hi."

"Yes." Tornberg stared at his shoes in a serious mood. "Chief Superintendent Markus Michelsson telephoned and asked me to let you know that Detective Inspector Harjunpaa and Detective Sergeant Harko are ordered to report in to his office as soon as possible."

"What on earth for?"

"He didn't specify."

Tornberg still looked serious but his eyes betrayed him: obviously he was vastly entertained by Michelsson's order. He nodded and disappeared.

Harjunpaa stood up.

"Can you guess why Tornberg didn't ring but came up here instead?"

Monica shook her head.

"He likes the spiral staircase. A couple of weeks back I found him sitting there, in the window recess, whistling to himself. You wait here. I won't be long."

Harjunpaa bounded downstairs. The whole thing

seemed more and more curious. Michelsson was one of the bosses in the larceny section and Harjunpaa had nothing whatsoever to do with anything in his department. Could it somehow be connected with the stolen car of the night before? But why, then, would he want to see Harko as well?

After a short search he found the right door and pressed the button. The yellow light came on, ordering him to wait. Harjunpaa put his ear close to the door. No sounds came from within. He shrugged his shoulders and leaned on the wall, thinking that possessing traffic lights at your door made you very important. In the old building only a few offices had been equipped with entry lights and the bosses had fought hard for the privilege of having a buzzer and three lights outside their doors. Then he thought that Norri might be free by now and that instead of wasting his time here he could have been checking muggings in Kontula. With irritation he pressed the buzzer again. The green light came on at once.

Michelsson was a tall, cylindrical man. Harjunpaa didn't know him particularly well, but he knew Michelsson had a reputation for being somewhat cranky. In the old offices he had habitually made notes of who used what cars, and when someone asked him why, he had replied secretively: "There'll be a good reason. There's no knowing what will be revealed one day." And still nobody knew. To his misfortune Michelsson had been a member of the team that planned the new building. Now that mistakes and howlers were coming to light he had become even more withdrawn and could be seen in the corridors only well before office hours.

Michelsson stood by the window, staring at the railway yard where a red diesel engine was busy putting a freight train together. He looked around to see who had entered, cleared his throat, but otherwise stood still, his back to the room.

"You wanted to see me?"

"Yes. We'll now see how honest you are. You and Harko were on night shift last Friday?"

"Yes."

Harjunpaa knew he'd done nothing wrong—and yet he felt uneasy. Had something disappeared—or had some relatives complained that all Nilsson's belongings hadn't been handed over?

"What were you eating that night?" Michelsson sounded perfectly normal but the back of his neck beneath the short hairline was turning red.

"What did I eat?" Harjunpaa was baffled.

"Yes. What did you eat? Did you, by any chance, have any eggs?"

"I . . . if you must know, I had nothing at all."

"And Harko, did he have eggs?"

"Not as far as I know."

It suddenly occurred to him that Michelsson might have flipped. He had been holding his hands behind his back, now he let them hang freely. Michelsson reeled around, his face set and angry.

"You are the last but one of the men working that night I have interviewed today. None of you had any eggs—or that is what you say. And yet, on Saturday morning, there were eggshells on the floor in the staffroom, in this new building. Can you tell me how it is possible that the same piggish ways go on in this new building as in the old?"

"I'm sorry but I don't think I can help you." Harjunpaa was out of the room in a flash and he slammed the door behind him.

The incident had so dumbfounded him that he had rounded a corner before he realized what he should have said: "Maybe it's because the same pigs work here in the new building as in the old."

12

Further to report RVA/R/15402/07

Investigators: Norri, Harjunpaa, Harko.

On Monday, 19th July, at 12:40, Nurse Anna Jarva (tel. 17371/263) reported that plumber Taisto Nilsson, (311045-073T) brought to the Surgical Hospital on Saturday, 17th July, had died. Nilsson was unmarried, registered as a resident of Agricola parish, home address Huvilakatu 3, 00140 Helsinki 14.

After he was admitted to the hospital Nilsson underwent extensive stomach operations. His injuries included several ruptures to the mesentery and to the intestines, ruptures to the liver, and hemorrhage of the stomach aorta.

At 10:20 on the date of this report a new operation was considered necessary due to suspected further hemorrhage. About 10 minutes after the operation Nilsson suffered heart failure. Attempts to resuscitate were not successful. Doctor Peter Olin certified Nilsson dead at 10:55

Since the death occurred while the subject was under hospital care and since it is believed that his injuries were not accidental or self-inflicted, the hospital has requested police help in establishing the cause of death.

At SUOPO this report is added to an earlier report, ref RVA/R/15402/07, attempted murder, investigator: Norri.

The deceased is transferred to the morgue. An autopsy will follow.

13

Kontula main road with its many lanes was a dividing line for the suburb. On its north side was an area of about two square miles that contained the shopping center and most of the high-rise blocks, built in precast concrete. The south side was low-lying land, the pine trees between the buildings as thin and weak as if growing on a marsh. There were several little copses that sheltered hovels put together by vagrants from bits of plastic and cardboard.

Furthest from the main road was a sports field, almost bordering on the next suburb, Mellunkyla. Beyond the sports field the land rose, becoming rockier. Joggers and those in search of a quiet spot to get drunk had worn the undergrowth full of crisscrossing paths—sometimes these followed an older track, covered with cobblestones, known as "cannon tracks." There were other things that supported the same military image: Along the cliffside was a collapsed trench, partly filled with rubbish; here and there some semicircular concrete bunkers remained, their openings smelling of dampness and mould; there were some metal bars fixed to the rocks, their function by now beyond memory and imagination.

At the edge of the cliff was a deep quarry, its area about the size of an average sitting room, with very high, steep walls. Its bottom was littered with all the rubbish a suburb can conceivably produce, including a small Fiat, beaten shapeless. At the edge of this quarry, kicking their heels, sat Mikael and Leo.

Between the boys was a plastic carrier bag holding eight unopened bottles of beer. On the rock around them were ten bottle caps, but no empty bottles.

"Look. Here goes another hand grenade!" Leo talked rapidly, as he always did when drunk. He threw a bottle, smashing it against the opposite wall, spraying foam and glass around.

"Fiuu-u . . . smash!" Leo blabbed. "Smashing! Wasn't that smashing, Miku?"

"Yes, yes. Don't push me or we'll both end up down there."

"Wouldn't that be smashing. All they would find of us would be some rags and bones, and they'd wonder who the hell it was."

"Don't."

Leo could not get Mikael going. This time even beer didn't help. He was drunk, quite nicely so—the boozy warmth spread from his belly, his hands were slow, as though they didn't belong to him, and when he closed his eyes he felt himself sway, like a mast on a ship. But his spirits could not be raised, they were barren, and all he wanted was to sit somewhere, quietly and alone.

The approaching night frightened him.

It was late evening already. The pink in the west was fading and the trees were growing darker.

He did not wish to stay another night in the cave. In spite of the campfire that had lit up their one corner, turning it into a red ball, it had been horrible, surrounded by deep darkness. And the smoke wouldn't go away, it stayed there, like a blanket, or a ghost, and made him feel they'd suffocate. Leo's tent smelled musty and there was only the one mattress, barely large enough for both of them. After a while you could feel how your clothes became dank and chilly.

Mikael hadn't slept well. His night had been a mixture of sleeplessness and nightmares. In his dreams he had been back in that police cell, Leo's cap on his head. The policeman had laughed: "That's it, your head has grown! Or have you got something inside the cap?" He had pulled the cap off and there was a thick snake inside. He chucked it into a corner, but the snake came back toward him.

Shivering with cold he had pressed closer to Leo, who slept and was warm. It had been so dark. He couldn't see, and the tunnel wasn't quiet, there were sounds. He had imagined how the snake was there, as wide as the tunnel, saliva dripping from its mouth. Then Leo had cried in his sleep, turned, and put an arm around him—that had made him feel better and he had then stayed awake, eyes open, till morning, thinking that being dead and buried must be like this—and then he was no longer afraid.

In the morning they had gone to the shops to get food and beer. A little later, when Leo's mum had gone out, they went in and took some clothes and two torches. The rest of the day they had spent on the rocks, sleeping in the sun. When he mentioned that Leo had put his arm around him in the night, Leo had gone quite mad and screamed he was no poofter.

"Hey, did you hear that, Miku? When they find our bones and put them together they mix them up and you'll get my legs and I'll get yours. And then they'll think that one was a chimp!"

"Not funny."

"Don't be so bloody wet! It's too dead here. We should speed things up, have some action, man. I know, we'll both have two beers, straight, and then we'll go to the shopping center and see some action. Yeah?"

"Yeah."

Leo opened four bottles. Then he gave a sign and they drank. The warm beer went down Mikael's throat, every mouthful making him more drunk. He felt better, somehow more confident. There was no need to worry about anything, things would work out. And then he got an idea: All he had to do was to pretend to pass out later on; then Leo would get fed up and leave him, and then he could go to Ulla's place and ask to sleep there, on the floor. Ulla would believe him if he told her that his father would beat him up if he went home.

Mikael finished his two bottles before Leo. Now that he'd made his mind up, he felt more at ease; now he wanted to be merrily drunk, like last Friday. He jumped up and shouted as loud as he could, "Yippee!"

The sound echoed around the mossy rocks and didn't die until it had reached the small private houses on the other side of the woods. Leo stood up as well.

"Let's go, Miku," he said eagerly. "I feel great. I want to see some bloody poofter trying to be clever. I'd give it to him, see, like this. I'd kick his face in. I'm good at kicking because I've got big feet. The other bloke, one kick and he was down!"

"Yeah, and got some stones on his belly!"

They left, the remaining bottles clinking in the bag.

Soon they reached the road that passed under the main road and led to the shopping center. They were walking fast, impatient to get there.

"But what if some of the gang are there?" Mikael said. "They're bound to start mouthing off. And you haven't got your cap or anything."

"Shit, that's true. My cap . . . but what the hell, let them, I'd like to have a fight with them, I'd show them who I am!"

"But what if my dad is there as well, by the door of the restaurant."

Leo stopped. His mouth was open and his eyes shone almost yellow.

"I tell you what, Miku. We'll give him a lesson. We'll hang around near your house. I'll make him get me back my cap."

"He's bloody strong," Mikael said uneasily. "And he's one hell of a mean pig. He's always on the lookout for someone to get at him. And he's always got his truncheon on him. He's got a special long pocket in his trousers for it—my mum had to make it for him."

"Shit. You can hide so he doesn't see you. And I'll go up to him and say I know where you are and you want to say you're sorry and go back home but you're too shit-scared. He's bound to come with me. And then, then I'll get him."

"But you'll let me have a go as well."

Mikael was gritting his teeth. His eyes felt tight.

"He's been beating me for so long," he said in a tense voice. "It's my turn now. I want to do it."

"I won't stop till he says he'll get my cap."

"But what if he snuffs?"

"Who cares. Then you can go back home."

"But you won't get your cap."

"True. We'll think about it."

They moved eagerly toward the bright lights of the shopping center. On the bridge above their heads the traffic was slowing down for the night. It was almost eleven.

Head cook Orvo Lagman lived in Kontula, in a detached red brick house. He hadn't bought the house, he had in-herited it from his parents. He had to struggle to keep up with all the expenses of living in a house like that; money seemed to melt away: There were rates, the oil bill, the garden was expensive to maintain, the drainpipes had to be renewed, and the downstairs windows were changed from double to triple. But a house of one's own was worth it, especially in Helsinki. And for the children it was ideal.

A little after midnight on Monday night—or rather, in the early hours of Tuesday—Orvo Lagman was not in

91

that red brick house of his, as would be expected. He was still on his way home.

He was traveling in a bus, quite drunk.

He had got drunk deliberately and very fast. He couldn't keep his head from nodding against the bus window, and when he tried to focus his eyes on something he could see amazingly clearly at first, but then the object would slide down and get blurred in double vision.

Orvo Lagman was ashamed. Not because there were other people in the bus; he was filled with remorse because of Pirkko and the boys. And maybe even because of himself.

How on earth could he have lost his temper like that?

It was quite rare for him to lose his temper at all. But this time he had really lost all control—and it had given him pleasure. All the way to the restaurant he had felt good about it. He had left the sauna without a word, didn't even shower, just pulled clothes over his sweating body. And the rest of the family had been too scared even to come after him until he was out on the porch, putting his sandals on. "Daddy! Where are you going?" Matti had been on the verge of tears. Had no doubt felt it was his fault. And Orvo had said, "I'm going to hell!"

Matti had cried. Petri had joined in out of sheer sympathy. And the baby had woken up and done her part, of course. Only Pirkko had remained quiet.

Orvo Lagman shifted his weight on the seat. He pressed his forehead until it hurt.

How could he . . . to a child? I'm going to hell. . . . How would he explain that to his son? And what would he say to Pirkko? Coming home drunk.

He felt ready to cry out of sheer frustration.

It had all started with such a silly, meaningless thing: Petri had demanded a plastic seahorse from Matti. It was Matti's seahorse, he had brought it to the sauna. He had every right to keep it. And yet, as a father he had ordered Matti to hand the thing over to Petri—otherwise Petri would have started a full-scale tantrum, with all the might of a three-year-old, and nobody would have got any joy out of the sauna. And it could be so nice, all of them there together—even Pirkko always became so soft and yielding in the sauna, she would come to his bed afterward, once the children were asleep, without having to be asked.

"I'm going to hell . . . damn it."

But Matti had not handed the toy over. Instead he threw it away, angrily, and quite by accident it landed on the hot stones, melting into a stinking mess. And then he was off.

The bus came to a sudden halt. Orvo Lagman was pressed against the window, then against the next seat. This must be a bus stop.

"Hey, man!" The driver had turned round and was looking at him. "You asked me to tell you when we get to Kontula. This is it."

"I see."

He pulled himself up and swayed to the door. The driver didn't say anything, although this door was strictly no exit.

"If you don't mind . . . could you tell me whereabouts in Kontula—"

"This is Kaarikuja."

"But I want to go to Panelian Road."

"Well, you'll have to walk. Might do you some good. It's only about half a mile. It's just as far if you go on to the next stop."

"I see."

"Well, are you getting out or not?"

"I'm going. Don't get mad. I'm going. Thanks very much."

The door closed with a swish and the bus rattled away.

Orvo Lagman took a deep breath—the night air felt

good, fresh. The queasiness in his belly was easing away, he was sobering up. And he knew why he had got so mad. It had nothing to do with that plastic seahorse. It was all to do with the way things were.

Nothing was drastically wrong, he wasn't unhappy or anything. But it was all so irritating. Their third one, the girl, was only four months old. She was so different, had constant colic, cried all through the night. She would start at midnight, as soon as he was back from work. He couldn't sleep. And Pirkko didn't get enough sleep, either, rocking the baby hour after hour in the sitting room.

Maybe they should have settled for two children. With Petri so big already they hadn't been tied down to specific feeding and sleeping times. For the first time they had been able to go to places, to do things together, as a family. Now it was all one big round of feeding bottles and pacifiers and inspecting rashes on the baby's bottom and running after the cheapest nappies on offer—and the boys were jealous, why else would they behave like that.

He came to the footpath that led to the pond, so deep in his thoughts that he didn't remember to turn right. Instead he carried straight on along the sandy path.

And then Pirkko didn't want it any longer. Well, what with his night shifts and the crying baby there wasn't much chance of it anyway. If only Pirkko could understand how he missed her, missed kissing her neck and thighs and tummy, so flat you would never guess she had borne three children. He missed her breath on his face and how she responded and dug her fingers in his back.

It wasn't as if he didn't like the baby . . . such tiny fingers . . .

He had to wipe his eyes. Everything would be all right once he got home and talked things over with Pirkko. And he would buy that go-cart for the boys, the one Matti had been whining about all summer; whatever the cost he'd get it.

He felt sober enough to want a cigarette. But he couldn't find any matches. He patted his pockets and looked around, confused. At first he couldn't think where he was, all he could see was bushes and stunted pines. He walked on and recognized the place: On his left was the playground, the one with the wooden frogs and the pond. Two boys were hanging round the frogs. He walked toward them, he'd ask them for a light and offer them a fag as well, if they were old enough to smoke.

"You know, that shit isn't going to turn up." Leo was sitting on a frog, pretending it was a horse.

"Maybe he wasn't there."

"What? How do you mean, wasn't there? You said yourself he'd be working in the restaurant tonight."

"I said he might be . . . or he might be in the police tonight. Or he could have gone somewhere to booze."

"Fuck you. You really are a dum-dum." Leo jumped down. His face looked smooth in a way Mikael knew to be dangerous, so he kept quiet.

"We've wasted the whole night because you're so dumb. Shit. We've been hanging round at least one hundred hours. And now you tell me. I'm really mad."

"It's not my fault if you don't listen to what's said."

"Dumb prick, you."

"Hi, boys."

Mikael started, jumped down. All night he'd been ready to hide on Leo's orders. But Sod had not come. The only fun all night had been when two small boys had come to play with a battery-powered boat. Leo had thrown a stone and sunk it. When one of the boys took his trousers off and went in to fetch the boat they had made him cry by laughing at his balls. The boys had threatened to get their fathers. Leo had said: "Why don't you, we sure want to kill someone." No father had come, nor anybody else to have a go at.

Mikael realized he had been startled for nothing. It wasn't Sod—even the voice was different. A total stranger was walking toward them. Drunk, couldn't even walk straight, but no bum. This had a neat jacket, tie, and all. His hair was standing up; it looked lacquered. When he came closer, stood next to them, he smelled of whiskey.

"Have you boys got a light? I must have lost mine somewhere."

"Yep."

Leo was digging in his pockets. It was always Leo who decided what was to be done and Mikael followed the lead, staying on the side, ready to bounce in.

"Are you brothers or what?"

"Yep. Dad's a policeman."

"I see. Thanks. Then you must be decent chaps. I have two boys myself. But smaller than you. And I have a girl too."

"You must be quite a man then, at least in that respect."

The man laughed.

"I suppose I am. But I'm a bit drunk at the moment. How do I get to Panelian Road?"

"We'll show you. We live that way. On Tuukkalan Road . . . you know the yellow house with the apple trees?"

"I don't . . . can't think which one right now. But how come you're out so late? Your brother looks quite young."

"We were taking our dog for a walk and it ran away. Only it isn't a dog, it's a tiger—one of those Sugar Frostie tigers, you know? The small yellow ones with blue stripes?"

"Whatever you say." The man laughed.

They started walking, all three. Leo was guiding them

96

toward the dense undergrowth and small pines. Mikael followed a few steps behind.

"Are you a poofter?"

Leo spoke abruptly, in a voice of intense loathing, as if he was feeling really sick.

"Me? Certainly not. What about yourself?"

"What! Are you saying I'm a fag? Did you hear that, Miku?"

Mikael was breathing fast. His hands were wet with sweat. He looked at Leo with wide eyes; Leo knew how to go about it. Leo called this teasing, he said it was more fun to beat someone when they were mad enough to fight back. And sure enough, when you felled someone who had been mouthing off to you, you felt better about it. He had asked for it.

14

Harjunpaa did not turn the light on in the room, only on the landing. He knelt by the bunk bed and held Valpuri's wrist. It was soft and warm, he could feel her pulse.

"Vallu, should you come for a pee?"

The girl had been whimpering in her sleep for a while. Now she sat up, her hair a wild tousle around her head. She reached her arms out and wrapped them around her father's neck. Harjunpaa lifted her up, tried to get the hem of the nightdress out of the way and ease the girl down on the pot. Valpuri would not let go of him or bend her knees, but a wide and mysterious smile spread on her face.

"Sit down, Vallu, sit."

The girl nodded her head but didn't make a move to sit down.

"Do you need to go?"

"Yes."

"Well, dear, do sit down."

Valpuri let go, went down like a stone.

Harjunpaa lifted her back to bed. The girl remained sitting up, still smiling.

"Put your head down now, it's time to sleep."

"Daddy."

"Yes?"

"Daddy."

Harjunpaa pressed her gently down.

"Daddy, you know what?"

"Yes?"

"Why don't we play together?"

"Valpuri. This is night. Go to sleep now. I've just got in, I'm going to bed, too."

"Yes. But we could go swimming, or to the big rocks."

"But only when it's day."

"Why?"

"But daddy promises, as soon as I have a day off . . . Vallu?"

The girl had gone back to sleep, quickly, before her father noticed.

Harjunpaa looked into the upper bunk. If Valpuri took after her mother, was soft and rounded, then Pauliina was more like her father with her long, skinny limbs, narrow face, and skin so transparent you could see her veins. Harjunpaa tucked in an arm that was dangling over the edge, that was all. Pauliina was seven already. Next autumn she would start school.

Harjunpaa crept to his bed quietly so as not to wake Elisa. He lay on his back, hands behind his head. He sighed, knowing that his mind would be activated as soon as he closed his eyes. It would be better to stare at the ceiling and let time pass, an hour, maybe two. He could hear the water filter in the aquarium downstairs, and the guinea pig munching its food. One of the girls turned in her bed, kicking the wall. Elisa didn't breathe like a sleeper.

"Timo."

"I thought you were asleep."

"No. Something wrong?"

"No. You remember Nilsson, he died today. And I went to the hospital to see him this morning."

"Oh."

"The whole evening was useless. We interviewed at least thirty youngsters at Kaisaniemi and at the station, waste of time. We had a look at Kontula—but what could we do? Should we start asking everybody if they by any chance have seen somebody drop a watch. You know, the whole place is full of kids hanging around, all hours."

"Really."

"I think soon we'll have no choice but to try and put pressure on both at the station and in Kontula, all the time, spend all day and all night there. Asking questions all the time. There will be no peace and in a week or so those whose business suffers when the police hang around just might get annoyed enough to find out some names for us."

Elisa was silent. The silence went on for so long that Harjunpaa thought she had gone back to sleep.

"Timo."

"Yes?"

"Don't you think it would be nice if we had three kids?"

Harjunpaa shifted. His thoughts were elsewhere. And besides, he found it hard to explain all his reservations. As it was he was worried about the people who might be a danger to his girls, more so as they grew older, became young women. He feared fast cars; once he had to interview a mother who had been left holding an empty mitten by the roadside, all that was left of her son. And he feared fanatics, thousands of miles away, who could press a button and turn living people into shadows on the ground. And he feared the battle they had to face for an opportunity to study or for a job—he had managed to step out of all that, he had become an observer who had to witness the daily toll of these battles.

He feared losing them, but would not admit that, not even to himself.

At times he felt that the responsibility for two young lives, just starting, was too much for him.

"Don't you think we are fine as we are—isn't it enough for us to see Paukku and Vallu growing up OK?"

"But you wouldn't be upset?"

100

"No, of course not. We could manage."

"Timo."

Elisa snuggled next to him. Her hand was warm. He turned on to his side and felt Elisa's legs. His arm slipped beneath hers, circled her back, he was close to her skin, breathing on her neck, near her ear. Very slowly he felt the world slip away. All that was left was this warmth.

15

"Kick," Harjunpaa said. The boy didn't make any move to get up, instead he tried to work out whether the man meant it. Then he looked at the wall.

"I might."

"Do. But I don't think you can."

The boy stood up and moved to the middle of the room. He was a pale-faced seventeen-year-old, not very beefy. His jeans had been bleached nearly colorless and over one thigh was written with a felt-tip pen: DON'T KICK ME OR I'LL KICK YOU. He had assaulted an off-duty soldier near the station on Friday night—he was one of those they were interviewing after checking all the reports for Friday—often one assault by a young person turned into a series of assaults. Harjunpaa, however, had a gut feeling that this boy had nothing to do with their case.

"There'll be a mark," the boy said. "A black mark. It's always black, doesn't matter what color the boots are."

"That's all right, you have my permission. But you must aim at the highest row of bricks."

"OK. I just thought this could be some plot or something . . . you trying to get me for something. Like pigs do."

"Never. Why do you say that?"

"The word gets round."

Harjunpaa didn't even have time to see how it actually happened. He sensed that the boy went tense, bent his knees slightly—and the next moment his foot went straight in the air, hit the wall, and then the boy was standing upright again. He had landed on one foot and both hands and bounced back up like a spring. Harjunpaa looked at the wall. Near the ceiling was a mark, curved, about five inches long.

"I told you. I could have made one that is like the whole sole . . . but when you do it like this you split the face open as well, it's sort of sharper, see, with more weight on the side. I told you I could've killed that soldier, if I'd wanted. All I did was give him a lesson, like."

"Are you a member of some club?"

"No. I was at first, but you had to be so careful there and not to hurt anybody. But I do practice, I go out and practice."

There was a knock, Norri appeared at the door. He looked quickly from the boy to Harjunpaa.

"Will you be long?" he asked.

"We're just about finished," Harjunpaa said, then turning to the boy. "If all this is correct, can you sign at the bottom of both pages?"

"OK. You're sure I don't get done for this?"

"Not for my case—or for this kick."

Only now did Harjunpaa realize that there had been something odd in Norri's voice. He looked up. Norri was fidgeting with his tie, straightening it unnecessarily.

"Now you know what sort of man I am," the boy said at the door.

"I do indeed. And next time someone gets kicked I know where to come with the leg irons."

"Ha, ha."

"We've got to go," the words burst out as if Norri had been holding his breath.

"It was a routine report, Cajander went to check. He's just asked for help through Central. He's certain the man was killed. The body is outside."

103

Harjunpaa had already pulled his jacket on. His thoughts raced—Cajander couldn't handle the case further, his section dealt with only deaths that were presumed natural. Because it was the holiday season there were only two chief inspectors in SUOPO at the moment, Norri and Sylvi Ursin—and she was in charge of the vice section. Harjunpaa suspected Norri's section would be landed with this new case although they already had an unsolved murder to clear. He opened a drawer, took out his gun and holster, and fastened them on his belt. Then he was on his way out, locking the door behind.

They walked briskly down the spiral staircase and down the corridor, toward the elevators, trying not to run. Someone had just made fresh coffee, its smell drifted in the corridor. Typewriters rattled behind closed doors. Someone was sobbing.

"The boys from the technical department are in the car already." Norri sounded as if his mouth was too dry. "Both of us had better go there—it's in Kontula."

A chill ran down Harjunpaa's spine. He opened his mouth, didn't say anything—there was nothing for him to say that Norri wouldn't have thought about already.

They reached the elevators. Harjunpaa pressed the button. He could hear the elevator on its way up. Tornberg came running from his office. He was breathless: "Norri, I rang the morgue, Monica's on the line now. She says they've only just started on the stomach. What'll I tell her?"

"There's someone from the technical department with them?"

"Ahlman."

"Tell them to leave it all to Ahlman. He can take notes as well as photograph. Give the address to Monica and Harko and tell them to get there as soon as possible."

"Right. I haven't been able to find Wallender yet."

"He can wait here when he turns up."

They stepped into the elevator and Harjunpaa pressed B for basement.

The car was waiting, engine running. Thurman had pulled up right outside the elevator doors—and yet he pretended to be yawning, and scratched his silvery-stubbled chin when the door opened. The sight of Norri made him sit up. He took the microphone and reported: "Central 8-9-1, for technical department and SUOPO. On our way to investigate suspected killing."

Norri got into the front, Harjunpaa shared the back with Ketonen, who was smoking quietly. Thurman stepped on the accelerator. Then he shoved his forefinger at the dashboard and the white walls of the garage changed color. It looked as if a blue fire was raging around them.

The car swerved around a corner and was outside in the sunlight. Thurman drove through Pasila, taking two right turns. "I'll take Koskelantie and then the road to Lahti. Faster than going through Kulosaari."

Norri coughed a small, dry cough. Harjunpaa looked out of the window. Cajander's voice came over the radio: "Central. Cajander calling."

Normally he was a calm policeman, expressing himself with deliberation. Now he sounded almost incoherent: "Tell the car on its way to Kontula to hurry up, and send one or two of your own patrol cars here, to help. Tell them to bring some sort of cover. There is quite a crowd over here, kids too, and I'm alone . . . it's difficult . . . not a very nice thing to see."

"Central signs. Car to Kontula, can you hear me?"

"8-9-1 is going flat out as it is!" Thurman shouted.

"3-7-4 can offer assistance," one of the regular patrol cars beamed in. "We have black plastic bags."

"Central signs 3-7-4 out."

The patrol car sent its "over and out," which drowned in the shrillness of sirens.

"Bloody hell," Thurman fretted. "They'll make the whole place useless with their messy feet!"

He thumbed another button. Through the roof came the first tentative cry, turning into a shrill, monotonous wail.

Norri was fumbling for his seatbelt. Ketonen squashed his cigarette in the ashtray and grabbed hold of the window frame. Harjunpaa held onto the sides of his seat as the speed pressed him back. The roadside greenery turned into a ribbon of fast-moving green patterns in his eyes.

16

The wailing subsided, then stopped altogether—except in the ears. There it went on, as if a swarm of irritated mosquitoes had been dancing around the head. Then other noises surfaced, the car engine and the sound of wind in the open windows. The lights were still flashing on the roof.

Thurman left the road to Lahti, turned right. The car was approaching Kontula. Norri took the microphone.

"Can Cajander hear Norri direct?"

"Cajander can hear."

"Can you tell me more precisely where you are? We're approaching along the Kontulankaari from the north."

"You're almost there! Turn off up a short road called Sakara Street. Carry on after the "no exit" sign, along the pedestrian way. A few hundred yards and—well, you'll see us."

Thurman was leaning forward, looking for the right street name.

"There!"

He braked abruptly and swung the car left, across the dual carriageway.

Sakara Street ended almost as soon as it had begun, widening out into a parking area between the houses. Ahead were low trees and behind them more houses. A narrow track, a path almost, led to the woods. Two young boys were pedaling frantically toward it; a woman in red slacks was running in the same direction. Thurman pressed the car along the narrow track, branches scraped the sides of the car. They reached a spot where the paths divided and a crowd of people had gathered. Behind the crowd the top of the patrol car was visible, its flashing light pale in the bright sunshine.

They parked behind the patrol car. Thurman and Ketonen reached for their kits, Harjunpaa and Norri jumped out. It was very hot, the midday sun shining directly down. They could smell trampled earth and plants, sweat and cigarettes, sickly scent. The crowd was babbling excitedly.

"There's the doctor now, wasn't in a hurry, was he?"

"They're from SUOPO."

"Lasse! Nip home and get the camera, quickly now!"

"Make way, please!" Norri shouted. It sounded odd. Harjunpaa couldn't remember ever having heard Norri raise his voice before. He pushed his way through to him, using his hands as if swimming between people, pressing the crowd away on either side.

"Police! Make way, please!" he shouted, beginning to feel angry. "Make way!"

"Don't bloody push."

"Joel! Come here. Have you seen my son? He's got a blue top and a toy car."

"Please make way for the police. Only those who have something to report should remain. The rest should disperse!"

Slowly they reached the trees. The back of Harjunpaa's shirt was soaked in sweat. Beads of sweat covered Norri's forehead. In the middle of the crowd was a uniformed policeman, his arms spread wide, trying to explain something. Another policeman was further away, his back to the newcomers, pushing a young man away, then turning around to grab a little kid trying to rush past his legs. Norri and Harjunpaa pressed on. There were people even up the trees, boys, some tiny toddlers, far too young to have managed the climb on their own; and, straddling a branch of a slender pine only about six feet up, was a fat man, well past middle age.

They pushed on through the crowd. In the middle there was a clear space, maybe ten yards across. The body was lying between some pines, covered with plastic. Only the legs were visible, as far as the knees. He wore brown sandals, white socks. The trousers had once been gray, but were now stained with soil and grass. Cajander was standing by the corpse, pressing his walkie-talkie to his ear. The wail of a siren drew closer from the direction of the town.

"I did my best." Cajander sounded frustrated. "But the crowd got here before me."

There was little need to say more—the earth had been packed hard, grass trampled, branches broken off; it would be a miracle if they could identify one single mark left by the killer. Norri waved his arm as if to calm Cajander, and moved toward the body. Cajander explained something to him in a low voice; Harjunpaa looked around. Only now did he realize how huge the crowd was—there must have been a hundred, maybe two hundred people. Most looked as though they were on holiday or retired, a lot of women, many carrying shopping bags, and children. The front row was silent but at the back people were chattering, some drunks were laughing.

Harjunpaa's hands were clenched. The anger he had felt a moment earlier was turning to hatred: These people just regarded the whole thing as something better than "Dallas," better even than a good booze-up, even preferable to a Cup Final or a new car with a fifth gear and rally stripes on the panels. Somehow he suspected that the man under the plastic covers was there for the sake of the very same things, was there because these things had become more important than life itself, more important than the time demanded by those kids in the front row, barely older than his Pauliina.

"Timo."

Harjunpaa moved across to Norri, automatically looking where he put his feet. Norri's lips were tight but his eyes had that familiar, deliberating look—Harjunpaa could imagine how Norri's thoughts were being marshaled, each evaluated in turn, weighed without the burden of any subjective considerations.

"Take a look at the sandals," he said in a low voice. Harjunpaa crouched down. The feet were together, one foot partly on top of the other. Harjunpaa was as startled as if he'd been slapped on the face—the sandals had been unbuckled, the straps crisscrossed and then rebuckled. Harjunpaa pulled his tie loose and opened the top button, a feeling of failure welling in his mind, souring everything. He stood up. The wailing sirens stopped somewhere near by.

Norri lifted the plastic. Disturbed flies buzzed as they flew up. Harjunpaa took only one look. He pulled his hand over his mouth as if to wipe sweat away. Norri pointed sideways—to a large rough stone. There was soil on its pocked surface and something else, too, fair strands of hair, moving in the light breeze.

"We have to clear this area before we can do anything." Norri was calm, talking like a mathematician who knew all the factors and which formulas were applicable. "But we'll never do it without help. Timo, you call Central and tell them we'll need at least ten, preferably twenty men to clear this area and fence it off. We also need as much marking tape as they can send us. Better let Varis know, tell him I'll call as soon as I can. Tornberg can start to draft a list of available investigators, but no point in sending any here. And a doctor—some patrol car can fetch him here. No need to involve the pathologist yet."

"Hey! Norri!"

Cajander had managed to remove a black wallet from the dead man's pocket without moving the body. He was holding it carefully between his nails. Harjunpaa moved toward the cars and now he didn't need to ask people to make way.

"Attention all!" That was Ketonen. He was using the loudspeaker in the police car; his voice sounded metallic as it echoed back from the nearest house.

"SUOPO investigator is fencing off this area. Everyone is requested to move immediately to the far side of the footpath. Those who don't do so will be prosecuted. I'll repeat that. . . ."

Harjunpaa met Monica and Harko.

"What does it look like?"

"We're still looking for the same killers," Harjunpaa replied tersely, and walked on.

Thurman had a roll of marking tape with him. He was tying it from tree to tree and people hastily scattered as he advanced. Harjunpaa saw Thurman stop beneath the man who had climbed up the short pine tree. He gave the tree a hefty kick.

"Get down." His voice was thick with annoyance. "Get down and scram if you are not a material witness."

"My shirt got stuck. This branch."

"Get down! It'll come off."

Harjunpaa heard Thurman venting his frustration on the tree trunk, then there was a shout of fear and a thump.

"I told you it would come unstuck."

Harjunpaa had barely got the microphone in his hand when there was a knock on the car window. A gray-haired woman in her sixties was standing by the car. She seemed so anxious that Harjunpaa opened the door.

"Yes?"

"Excuse me, could you tell me . . . if it's our Juho?"

Harjunpaa thought that he should have waited to see the contents of the wallet. The woman was fingering a

111

cross that hung from her neck. Her fingers were fat and nervous, her eyes painfully wide.

"Do you have some reason to think it might be?"

"He went out last night. And hasn't come back home yet. Father and I . . ."

Tears welled up in her eyes and rolled down her cheeks.

"Can you tell me what Juho looks like."

"He's sort of blond. Thirty-two. With a small moustache and blue eyes, a short stubby nose."

Harjunpaa looked down at his hands; the large stone had hit the dead man's face, maybe more than once—there was no face any longer; beneath that black plastic there was only congealed blood and bits of broken bone, an eye torn off, a gray mess.

"What was he wearing?"

"He had a shirt on, with printed flowers. And blue velvet trousers."

"It's not your Juho," Harjunpaa said in a low voice. "He was someone else's, he had gray trousers."

"Thank you, thank you so very much!"

She was crying openly but smiling at the same time. She touched Harjunpaa's hand lightly and waddled quickly away. Harjunpaa rubbed his face. He felt ashamed, ashamed because a moment ago he had hated these people—they couldn't help it, after all, only an arbitrary decision by some lawmakers decided when you were no longer a child and became an adult.

Harjunpaa lit a cigarette after he had conveyed all his messages. He didn't have time to get out of the car before Norri joined him, the wallet in his hand. He climbed in and closed the door.

"It seems the victim was Orvo Lagman, head cook—as you saw we can't identify him by his photograph. He lives quite near by, in Panelian Road. We have to find out if it really was him."

Norri put the driving license down. In the photograph Orvo Lagman had a roundish face, fair, wavy hair, blue eyes; his smile was forced. Norri took out another photograph. It was not very recent, or at least it had been in the wallet for some time; it was worn. The photograph showed a slim, dark-haired woman sitting on a garden swing, holding a small child in her lap. By the swing stood a boy, maybe six years old, clutching a hobby horse. Norri turned the photograph over. Somebody had drawn a red heart on the reverse side and written inside it: "Pirkko, Matti, & Petri—my precious darlings."

Harjunpaa stared at the end of the house behind the trees.

"Why don't you go?" Norri suggested. "Cajander said you could take his car."

Harjunpaa inhaled deeply, and held the smoke in before answering: "Well, I'd better be off then."

Harjunpaa parked the car half on the pavement and turned the visor down, displaying a piece of paper with a black P and an official stamp on it, reinforced by some indecipherable signature. He looked out of the window at the house. It was of red brick, its roof painted green. Lilacs and some other shrubs he couldn't name grew in the garden.

Then he stared at the dashboard for quite a long time, without moving his gaze.

He could feel something go hard inside, die a little. This was not a new experience, it had happened hundreds of times and he knew it would happen again and again. He opened the door abruptly and got out. He didn't want to think too far ahead, not to think what would be left when too many of these little deaths had occurred.

He opened the red gate and walked down the concrete slabs which formed the garden path. The garden was

113

tidy, well tended, the lawn thick and smooth, and the borders carefully weeded, exposing soft black earth under the bushes. To the left was a sandbox, toys in a neat pile in one corner. Outside the front door was a tricycle—Valpuri had one just like it, even the rubber handlegrips were broken in the same way—only this one was blue while Valpuri's was yellow.

Harjunpaa walked up to the door. The nameplate was in copper, old-looking. The name Lagman was engraved in curved script. Harjunpaa pressed the bell and heard the ding-dong inside. He felt for his wallet and pulled out his badge.

Nobody came to the door. He couldn't hear any sound from the house—no steps, no noise of children. He took a deep breath and rang the bell again, although by now he was pretty sure that there was nobody in. He waited a little longer before turning away. He felt a distant relief; it was like a dream he couldn't quite recall but knew he had seen.

He intended to go straight back to his car but on an impulse he sat down on the doorstep instead. He decided to wait a while; maybe the Lagmans would come back soon. He knew he ought to go straight back to Norri and the others, he was sorely needed there, in learning what there was to learn from the body, in finding out who among the onlookers actually knew something, in having a word with the youngsters, in mapping out the area where they should start interviewing—but instead he sat in the sun, on the doorstep, listened to bees making their rounds of the lupins, and stared at his official police badge.

"This police officer is Detective Inspector Timo Harjunpaa from Helsinki police force."

"Hey! What are you doing in there?"

A thin woman was standing behind the hedge. She might have been there for quite a while already—her

114

face looked suspicious and she kept glancing over her shoulder, as if waiting for reinforcements from her own house. Harjunpaa stood up.

"I'm waiting for the Lagmans. Have you any idea where they might be?" ·

"They went to town, maybe an hour ago. She drove, they even had the baby with them."

"What about Orvo? I mean Mr. Lagman? Did he go as well?"

"Of course not. Or else she wouldn't have been driving."

"Did they mention when they would be back?"

"No they didn't. That's none of my business. And is it any of yours?"

Harjunpaa said nothing. They stared at each other.

"Are you some sort of rep?" she asked finally.

"Sort of."

"What sort?"

Harjunpaa shrugged his shoulders.

"Well, whatever it is you're selling," she was clearly affronted, "we buy nothing. Neither do the Lagmans. We've all agreed that we've nothing to do with any reps or any other sort of callers. We want our privacy, we want to keep ourselves to ourselves."

She turned to go. As she went she muttered something in a discontented voice.

Harjunpaa made his way toward the gate.

17

"You mean Sid Vicious?" The girl looked up quickly, met Harjunpaa's eyes, and turned to her friends again, ready to burst into giggles. She was maybe fourteen, thin and angular. She pulled her shoulders back so that her small breasts stuck up under her blouse; she might have been pretty had her face not been covered excessively with makeup, and had she not been chewing gum so vigorously that her jaw seemed in danger of dislocation.

"Yes."

"Dunno . . . or yeah, sure I know!"

Harjunpaa shifted his weight from one foot to another. But he didn't allow himself too much hope—he could guess what he would hear next.

"You must go to England if you're after Sid Vicious," she said. "You see, that's him in them videos."

"OK. Thanks a lot."

The whole gang was laughing—hard, brittle laughter, which carried along the shopping center walkways and made people turn to look.

"Let's go, Timo," Monica said in a low voice. "We can take a break while the crowd here changes."

They headed toward the car park and their Lada. The first ten paces Harjunpaa walked with brisk annoyance: He was well used to foul language, used to almost any other response, but not to the derisive snigger they had met time and time again that night. Its message was that what they were trying to do was considered totally unimportant by the people they had been talking to. All the same he hadn't given up hope yet—after all, this was the first night they were combing Kontula knowing what it was they were looking for.

The previous day had produced far more results than they had dared to hope—and especially the scene of crime had yielded more than expected. A metal detector had recovered a silver pendant on a broken chain under the trampled undergrowth. The pendant, shaped like a razor blade, had an inscription: SID VICIOUS. The pendant had not come from any of the shops in Kontula. The importer had provided them with a list of stockists in Helsinki—within a day or two they should find the shop that had sold it.

Thurman had kept a jealous eye on the police surgeon. When he had wanted to have the body turned over, Thurman had told him to stop. And his hunches had paid off: When the body was lifted, footprints were revealed. Some were made by jogging shoes similar to the ones they had recorded in Kaisaniemi; some were made by narrow shoes, possibly with leather soles.

During the preliminary interviews they had discovered three people (two had been walking a dog, the third was returning from a late shift in a sweet factory) who had passed the place around midnight. All had noticed two boys near the frogs. The woman who was coming home from late shift had got an earful of obscenities from the boys and had made the most detailed observations: One of the boys had been tall and hunched, the other short and very fair. Both had been drinking from a bottle.

The pond was drained. In the bottom, among other rubbish, were four broken beer bottles; from the children's sandbox the police had retrieved four caps that had been wrenched from the bottles with the aid of something other than a bottle-opener. There were no fingerprints left, either on the bottles or on the caps.

117

The police had spent all Tuesday night in Kontula—all the houses near the footpath had been checked. Showing a photograph of Orvo Lagman, they had posed the same questions at hundreds of doors:

"Were you out last night? Where? At what time?"

"Have you ever seen this man?"

"D'you know of a boy round here who's known as Sid Vicious?"

"Can you think of any two boys, around fifteen, who hang around together, one tall and stooping, the other short and fair?"

Once it was too late to ring any more doorbells they had continued round the streets and in the shopping center.

That same night they had finally got in touch with Orvo Lagman's wife. She had turned up at the police station with her brother-in-law, to report a missing husband; but she could not say where her husband had been the previous evening. The bus ticket they had found in the dead man's pocket had led them to a bus driver who remembered Lagman well and had been positive that he had left the bus on his own.

All Wednesday was spent checking information and continuing interviews. Now, at nearly 9:00 p.m., Harko and Wallender were at the railway station, asking questions about Sid Vicious, while Monica and Harjunpaa were similarly occupied in Kontula.

Harjunpaa chucked his cigarette out of the car window. It sent off sparks as it hit the tarmac. Now that he had a chance to sit for a while, unoccupied, the same feeling he'd had a couple of times earlier that day returned to him: he felt there was something he knew but didn't connect correctly, something that fitted together with something else—and again his mind played back a scene from a TV program of Kenny Everett and his parody of

118

Sid Vicious, dressed in studded leather jacket and a peaked cap.

Monica switched the engine on.

"Better take a longer break from this and nip back to
the office," she said. "Norri might well have got something new for us."

Harjunpaa raised a finger. He looked baffled.

"Think, Monica," he said slowly. "Where did we come
across a tall boy and a short one . . . quite recently?"

Monica turned the ignition key again and the engine
died. Her eyes were narrow and she was frowning.

"I can't remember," she said. "And yet . . . it's like
being in a shop and knowing that there's something else
you want to buy, only you can't remember what."

"Those kids who stole that Anglia!"

"True. And didn't Central say that the car was stolen in
Kontula?"

"That Sid Vicious on TV has a peaked cap. And you
remember what was on the ground, there, on the other
side of that fence?"

"Hell, Timo."

They sat still. Harjunpaa could feel how the realization
made his flesh creep. For a moment his thoughts jostled,
one following hard upon another; then they began to set-
tle down—and with order came the doubt, as usual.

"The one we got, his father is a policeman."

"Really? I didn't know."

Harjunpaa dug out cigarettes for them both.

"Well, what does that prove?" Monica was blunt. "Just
consider the facts. Besides, I once arrested a boy whose
father was a parson—he and two of his mates had raped
a music teacher. What was that boy called?"

"Bergman, Mikael Bergman. And they live in Vesala,
next to Kontula."

"We can check the address with Central and go round there at once."

"Yes."

Harjunpaa rubbed his chin. He well remembered Bergman *père*'s attitude. And what the duty officer had told him about his background. His mind's eye could still recall the boy slumped on the bench in the interview room—a small, pitiful creature with a childish face and eyes full of anxiety and an urge to tell. Harjunpaa dragged on his cigarette. He couldn't think of a pretext to call at the house without making Bergman suspicious.

"Better not rush into it," he said at last. "I think we should check round first. Look, how about if we ring them up. We shall know a lot if they can tell us where Mikael was on the night before last. I wouldn't be in the least surprised if Bergman had chained him to his bed."

"OK, there's a telephone over there, next to the taxi rank."

"There can't be too many with a name like that around here."

Harjunpaa stepped out into the warm night air: It was still almost too hot. It had turned dark unusually early. During the afternoon black clouds had started to gather on the horizon. Harjunpaa could hear some distant rumble but couldn't tell if it was an airplane or thunder. He opened the door of the telephone kiosk.

There were two columns of Bergmans, seven Nils Bergmans, but only with the right-sounding address. Harjunpaa put a coin in and dialed.

"Bergman."

It was a woman's voice. Harjunpaa remembered how Mrs. Bergman had followed him to the door, wanting to ask something; he shifted his feet uneasily, tried to do some quick thinking and asked: "Is Mikael at home?"

He felt he had chosen the wrong way after all. She was

silent for a few seconds, then said: "No. . . . Who's calling?"

"Detective Inspector Harjunpaa, good evening."

"Good evening."

Harjunpaa sensed that she was becoming even more cautious—or else her breathing was uneven, as if she'd had to run to answer the phone, or had been crying.

"I only wanted to check a few things about that stolen car," Harjunpaa said. "But I can just as well call back tomorrow."

"No point," she said. "Mikael's with his grandma in the country. We took him there that night. My husband . . . it's a punishment, he'll have to stay there till school begins again."

"I see. . . ."

"You can't ring him there, my mother's not on the phone. Mikael's there, in Nastola. . . . But I understood that the person in charge of that car case promised . . . I thought Mikael doesn't have to . . . that all the paperwork is sorted out?"

"Yes, I only wanted to check a few points. Thank you very much."

Harjunpaa put the receiver down. He wondered what he would say if some policeman rang Elisa and asked in a roundabout way questions about him or the girls.

"Oh, hell."

Monica's eyebrows were quizzical.

"Well?"

"No luck."

Harjunpaa slumped in his seat, he felt both disappointed and relieved at the same time.

"That was his mother. They carted the boy to his grandma on Sunday night, as a punishment. He's in Nastola."

"Well, that's that then," Monica sighed. "Mind you, I

was thinking how I would feel if someone came to tell me that Mikko . . . but you never know, especially the parents often don't know the first thing, many don't even want to know."

"We can find out who the other joyrider was—he can still be the right one; perhaps he had a different mate this time."

"Can any of Norri's team hear me, this is Central calling."

Harjunpaa grabbed the microphone.

"This is 8-2-5, Nisonen and Harjunpaa. We're in Kontula shopping center, just about to return to the office."

"Good. There are some customers who want to talk to someone about that Kontula case. Norri's in the middle of an interview and he already has someone else waiting."

"We're on our way. Ask somebody to take them to a waiting room."

Monica started the engine and turned the car out to the road. Harjunpaa raised the microphone to his lips once more: "What kind of customers?"

"They tell me a man with two boys. Is that enough?"

"Yes. Thanks."

Monica checked the rear mirror and changed gear. Again there was a distant rumble, but not a single streak of lightning could be seen.

18

"Well, boys?"

"You see, Tom and me went to play with the boat."

"It's my big brother's."

"Yes," Harjunpaa coaxed, and the father of one of the boys, the one called Harri, said again in the same apologetic voice as earlier on in the elevator: "I hope we're not taking up your time for nothing—you know how kids talk . . . but when our mother said that the police had called from door to door."

Harjunpaa waved his hand reassuringly and nodded to the boys. Both were barely nine years old. Harri was holding a white plastic carrier bag that contained something large and sharply angular.

"Yes, and then?"

"We were at that pond near our house, that's where that man was killed. But when we got there two bigger boys were there already and we thought we wouldn't go after all."

"They were on the other side, where the frogs are."

"But then we thought they'd soon go anyway, see they were sort of waiting and looking at the road all the time. We wanted to see the lights in the boat, in the dark . . . so we went and put it in."

"The lights were really great."

"And then the boys came over. The tall one said to let him control it—that's because he thought it was radio-controlled . . . we said you can't, it just comes back on its own. But he got mad and said he'd show remote control."

"And he threw a stone and the boat went to the bottom."

"But you could still see the lights."

"Yes."

Harjunpaa took his pen and fiddled with it. On the way in he had allowed himself to hope that one of the boys would be tall, one short. Now the initial disappointment had vanished and he had to force himself not to reveal to the boys how excited he was. Monica sat by the door, rocking her foot.

Harri lifted his bag onto the table and dug out a boat. It was mainly white plastic but the deck looked like real wood. The lights were like little drops of glass, green, white, and red.

"That's where the stone hit, see, there's a crack. And the engine got wet and it doesn't go no more."

"Shame."

Both boys had their eyes glued on Harjunpaa. He had a vague impression that they expected him to perform some miracle and make the boat good again. He touched it lightly with a fingertip.

"And what happened then?"

"I took my trousers off and went in to get it. It belongs to Marko, that's my brother. He would've gone spare . . ." his voice petered off and he stared at the floor.

Then Harri said, "He's real stupid, he took his underpants off, too. And them boys started to shout that he's a girl since he's got no . . ."

"Never. Did they say anything else?"

"When Tom had fetched the boat we said we'll get our father. And they said yeah, and that they'd want to kill him."

124

"No they didn't. They said they wanted to kill some-body anyway."

Harjunpaa stared at his hands. He didn't even dare to glance at Monica. A door opened somewhere along the corridor as somebody left Norri's room. Air-conditioning hissed high up near the ceiling.

"What then?"

"We didn't fetch our father because he wasn't in."

"Yes. What else?"

The boys shrugged their shoulders.

"Did you notice what time it was?" Harjunpaa tried again.

"It was late, you see we had to wait for it to get dark, to see the lights. Must've been eleven."

"A little late for boys of that age, I know," Harri's father said, avoiding Harjunpaa's eyes. "But we've said that it's OK in summer. It's so hard to force them . . . and since Tom can stay out till twelve, we felt it would only be fair."

"Yes," Harjunpaa replied, studiously avoiding Monica's eyes. But he could hear how she shifted her chair, scraping it against the floor.

"Can you tell me what these boys looked like?"

"That Leo is really tall. He's almost as tall as our dad, but much thinner. He's got jeans and jogging shoes and a sort of waistcoat. . . ."

"Just a moment," Harjunpaa cut in. "You said one of the boys is Leo. D'you know them?"

"I know Leo. Or I've seen him. He lives in that very big block opposite ours. On the other side of the trees."

"I think that would be Number 3 in Kotikonnuntie." The father's voice sounded proud; he had noticed how keen Harjunpaa was.

"D'you know his surname?"

"No. But the other one's Doman. At least once Leo said

125

to him: 'You Doman.' But we don't know him at all. He was sort of not so bad. But Leo's really awful. Everyone's afraid of him. He's always doing something horrible. He's got a razor blade hanging on his neck and once when we were playing on the rocks he said he'd cut our heads off with it if we didn't clear off."

Harjunpaa pulled an interview form from his drawer. His fingers were so sweaty that the paper stuck on them.

"OK. Why don't we put this on paper now while we're at it." He spoke as casually as he could. He realized that on no account must he excite the boys; he knew how easily tales could be elaborated to please the listeners even better.

An hour later Harjunpaa had taken the man and the two boys down to the front door. Monica and Norri were waiting in his office when he returned to the fifth floor. Small, red spots burned on Monica's cheeks.

"Look at this, Timo."

She pushed a piece of paper at Harjunpaa. It was a copy of a crime report.

JHE/R/9854/MTO 3300. Received by Sandvik. Investigator: Lund. Reported by: Rissanen, Tuomas, housing manager in Kontula flats.
Category: Criminal damage
Time of event: Sat. 17/07/this inst./about 02.30-03.20
  Details: Rissanen reported that in one of the houses under his supervision, Number 3, Kotikonnuntie, the upper one of the two glass windows in the door leading to staircase K, size approximately 45 × 50, had been broken during the above-mentioned time by a stone thrown through the window. The stone, appr. 10 × 7, was later found in the corridor and was handed to the police when the incident was reported.
  When interviewing the inhabitants housing manager Rissanen had established: Old-age pensioner Risto Molander who lives off the above-mentioned staircase K in flat 121, had been woken at the relevant time by shouting in the front of the house. When he looked out of the window he saw a youth outside. This youth he recognized

as one of the inhabitants of the same staircase. The youth, who is tall and stooping, was holding in his hands something that might have been a stone. Soon afterward there was the sound of breaking glass. Molander did not see the youth outside again after this.

Cook Marjo Ignatius who lives in Number 123 had been woken by the sound of breaking glass and when looking through the spy-hole in her door, she had observed a youth whom she recognized as Leo Melin, unemployed, who lives in the flat 198 off the same stair-case.

Housing manager Rissanen demands appropriate punishment once the suspect is found guilty and also demands costs to be ordered according to a bill to be submitted.

The suspect is Melin, Leo Johan, Kotikonnuntie 3 K 198, 00940 Helsinki 94.

Harjunpaa took a deep breath and let his hands fall down to his sides. A rare smile played around Norri's mouth. Monica looked lively and excited.

"I remembered something when that boy mentioned the name Leo, it's not all that common." Monica spoke quietly, as if for fear of disturbing something. "And all the time you were interviewing them I was trying to re-member where I had seen it. And then I got it. It was on Harko's desk, fourth down in his tray, and would have surfaced in a day or two. Harko would've gone to inter-view him or would have called him in here."

They stood silently for a moment, staring at each other. Then Norri cleared his throat. "We must go at once. Where's the rest of the team?"

"All out, somewhere around the station. There was a radio message that said they were after someone called Lundberg who had had blood on his trouser legs on Tuesday morning."

"Will you ask Central to call them back here. Or rather, to send them straight to Kontula. You can fix a place where to meet. And Monica, you check if we have any-thing on this Melin. Bring along anything you find, espe-cially any photos. I'll get someone to let you into the house in Kontula. And maybe we should start sorting out the Domans who live thereabouts."

Harjunpaa didn't follow the others out of the room immediately. Somehow he knew it would all be over soon. But he wasn't relieved. Somewhere at the bottom of his mind unease stirred, quite distant still and so shapeless he couldn't give it a name. His skin felt cold and clammy and he realized he was staring at the mark near the ceiling, made by a shoe, the mark of a kick.

He turned around, opened the bottom drawer, took out a tear gas spray, shook it, and dropped it into his breast pocket. Then he took a pair of handcuffs and was slipping them through his belt when his eyes happened on a photograph in the bottom of the drawer—a photograph he never displayed on his desk, one of the girls sitting by the Christmas tree. Valpuri was smiling but Pauliina was sucking her lip and looking disgruntled. He pushed the drawer to and stood up, not wanting to face that photograph any longer. He hesitated, then bent down and reopened the drawer, picked out one lead bullet, took his revolver, opened the drum and dropped the bullet into the nearest chamber, the one the hammer would hit first.

Only then did he pick up the receiver and dial Central.

19

Harjunpaa switched the lights off before he guided the car into the car park. He parked between a Renault 4 and an old Amazon, as near the end of the block as he could make it. Only a few blue street lights punctured the darkness.

"Central, 8-2-5 calling." Monica held the microphone close to her lips and spoke almost in a whisper.

"This is Central."

"Have you got through to Harko and Wallender yet?"

"No reply yet. But the call is out."

Monica's tongue darted over her lips. She gave Harjunpaa a sideways look.

"Does Norri know what the situation is? What does he say?"

"Hold on, I'll check."

Harjunpaa took out cigarettes for both of them. The burning ends were reflected in the windscreen like two red eyes.

"8-2-5, do you hear me, this is Central. Norri says stay put and keep surveillance on the staircase. If we don't get Harko within a quarter of an hour we'll send a patrol car to assist you."

"All clear. Over and out."

Harjunpaa looked at the block of flats. The gable end was dark and unrelieved by any windows, so high that he couldn't see the top.

"Where the hell are they," he whispered. "I bet the

caretaker isn't going to hang around with the keys for the rest of the night. . . . Monica, I tell you what we'll do. I'll go and ask him to leave the door unlocked. And I'll go in, I'll go one floor above, to the sixth. You stay opposite, behind those trees. If he's in and goes out I'll give you a warning and come down after him. And if he's coming in, you warn me first and then come in a little later yourself. I won't let him into the flat. I'll . . . I'll take him at the elevator door. OK?"

Monica didn't reply. She looked somewhat displeased and gave Harjunpaa a hard look.

"Norri told us to keep a surveillance on the staircase, nothing else," she said.

"Well, that's what we're doing."

"OK, as long as you remember just that. And don't try anything up there at the flat door."

"As if I would."

Harjunpaa turned to take a walkie-talkie from the back seat. He didn't consider himself foolhardy—nobody dealing with violent crimes did. The last one to try heroics had been buried twenty years ago. Harjunpaa had heard the story, how he'd tried to take an armed managing director by surprise, by diving down and grabbing him by the feet.

The walkie-talkie required him to punch a longer series of numbers to get through to the network than the car radio. Harjunpaa frowned and picked up the microphone from its holder.

"Central, 8-2-5 is dividing. We can be reached through walkie-talkies. Call for Monica or Timo. Will you let Harko know about this when you reach him?"

"Monica or Timo. Over and out."

They left the car. It still wasn't raining. The night air was stagnant and unpleasantly muggy; humidity was like a thin film that clamped on the skin. Harjunpaa chucked Monica the car keys. There was nobody about. Cars

130

drove past in the distance, beyond the houses; mopeds somewhere nearer. Somewhere in the high wall above them a window was open and Abba was singing "I do I do I do" in full throttle.

Harjunpaa touched Monica's hand; her fingers were cold and trembled slightly.

"Monica, you go round that corner. Stop roughly opposite their staircase. When the others turn up you explain the situation and tell them both to come up—we'll try then to get into the flat."

"What about me?"

"You wait here. Someone has to make sure he doesn't come up and surprise us."

Monica's eyes were narrow. She was about to say something, changed her mind, and whispered instead, "Fair enough. Take care."

Then she was off, with purposeful steps, shoving the walkie-talkie into her shoulder bag—Harjunpaa knew that her revolver and the short rubber truncheon were there already.

The caretaker was waiting at the front of the building. He was a young, broad-shouldered man; judging by his manner obviously fresh from the army.

"Are you looking for someone in connection with our murder?" he asked.

"In a way, might be a witness."

"Is it true? If you're after the killer I'll come along, I'd show him that he's nothing special. I'd stuff him down the lavatory before I'd hand him over to you. I could give him such a beating that—"

He stopped abruptly, realizing to whom he was talking.

"What I mean is . . . it makes me sick . . . some of my mates told me, who'd seen the geezer. You wouldn't believe it, arms and legs hacked off, stomach split open and guts stuffed into his mouth."

"Well, thanks for the trouble you're taking. Please,

131

don't hang around here waiting for something to happen."

The staircase was silent and depressing. The concrete corners were sharp, with bits broken off. The only color in sight was gray. The board that listed the residents on that staircase hung on the wall; it was a long one. Melin was listed on the fifth floor, as he had expected. Harjunpaa pressed the elevator button and started to climb the stairs.

He was out of breath when he reached the fifth floor. He knew he smoked too much and had made many attempts to stop. He could keep it up for a month; then he got depressed, felt he had lost a shield that had protected him against the rest of the world.

The door to Melin's flat was to the far right, by the stairs leading up. Harjunpaa stopped to get his breath back. Only now did he realize he'd forgotten to ask the caretaker to give him a key to the flat.

"Oh hell."

He pressed his fingers on his forehead. He could see how Harko and Wallender would race up the stairs and wait eagerly for him to open the door.

Harjunpaa decided to check the door, in case the fit was bad enough for him to slip a lever in. He stepped closer. Light shone around the letterbox as if it wasn't fastened to the door at all. He could hear sounds from inside the flat—the rustle of clothing, hasty steps, somebody bumping against a piece of furniture. Harjunpaa squatted and pushed the flap gently with his fingertips. The whole contraption moved with a sharp click. Harjunpaa bit his lip, waited; he was sure they could easily pull the letterbox out and then reach inside to turn the lock. Nobody came near the door. Harjunpaa knelt down.

The hall was a narrow one. Propped against the opposite wall were five bags of rubbish; between the bags were squashed beer cans. In the middle of the floor was a

132

long, white cardigan. The draught brought stale air to his nostrils, mixed with a recent spray of scent or deodorant.

Somebody came from the sitting room, a woman. That had to be Leo's mother, Kaarina Melin—according to the house register only those two lived in this flat. It seemed to Harjunpaa that she'd just got in. Now she bent toward a mirror, used some makeup on her cheeks, rubbed them lightly—obviously she was on her way out, after all. She had just popped in then, maybe someone was waiting for her to return, in a restaurant, in some other flat.

Harjunpaa barely realized what was happening before she had already scooped up the cardigan, the light switch was pressed, and the scene went dark. Harjunpaa had time to get up but not to move away from the door before the lock clicked and the door was pushed open.

"Good grief."

"Good evening, excuse me. I was just about to ring the bell. I am Detective Inspector Harjunpaa from SUOPO. Is Leo at home?"

The woman pressed her hands over her breasts, retreated, bumped into something. Harjunpaa stepped in and switched the light back on. Then he felt for the cold metal of his gun. He listened but could only hear the woman's moaning, no other sounds in the flat. Harjunpaa remembered that she had not spoken to anyone while he had observed her—and that she had left the flat in darkness. All the same he was cautious, still remembering the unease he had felt back in his office.

"What d'you want with that wretch this time?" She spoke in a pitiful voice, propping herself against a wall. She was drunk, far more so than Harjunpaa had realized at first—her eyes were moist and glazed and you could tell she had difficulty in focusing.

"Police about the place all the time. Are you going to take him in?"

"At this stage we want to interview him."

133

"Interview? Shit!"

She rushed forward, lost her balance, and grabbed Harjunpaa by the arm—he could smell musk and vermouth.

"You lock him up!" she shouted, her face turning ugly. "You lock that beast up so that I can have some rest . . . there's no peace . . . he's at me all the time! He takes it all! Money and booze and food, he takes blankets from my bed! I can't . . . I can't take it any more!"

Harjunpaa closed the door to keep the noise within the flat. He shook his arm free. Looking at the woman's face he could tell she was working herself up, but he couldn't understand why; he suspected it might be to get him out of the flat. Keeping his fingers close to the revolver, he tried to see past her into the other room.

"OK, if you can tell me where I can find Leo. . . ."

"Where you can find him? How the hell would I know? Not here, that's for certain. Leo! Are you here?"

Harjunpaa pushed past the woman, slipped into the sitting room, switched the lights on. There was nobody in the room. An unmade bed, sheets twisted into graying ropes, a table covered with bottles and full ashtrays, something spilled all over the surface. The woman came in after him, laughing. She sounded flat, totally joyless, there wasn't even mockery in her laughter. Harjunpaa rushed to the door that lead to a kitchenette—the sink and the cooker were heaped full of dirty dishes; on the floor lay a green bowl, shattered, dried food amongst its pieces. The refrigerator was humming noisily.

Harjunpaa turned around. The woman had lifted a bottle to her lips, was gulping down the last dregs. Harjunpaa kept his eyes on the door on the opposite wall. There was at least one more room to the flat.

"I mean it, lock him up." The rage had gone out of her, she sounded almost indifferent. "He's the same as his father, a criminal. It was his father who took him out

134

on a job for the first time, they stole some oak paneling from a timberyard in Herttoniemi, knew someone who could use it. And now Jussi rots in some clink in Sweden, who knows where—Johan Melin, there was a fine father for little Leo. And the clink is the right place for the boy as well, he deserves it."

"Have you no idea where he could be?"

"I suppose he must sleep somewhere, I'm not interested in bums like him. . . . But he does come here almost every night, always to take something—food and booze and clothes. I've told him time and time again to clear off, to go. But not him. He hangs onto me like some bloody babe in arms and spoils everything for me."

"D'you know who his mates are?"

She tossed her head, making her dyed red hair fly around her face.

"How the hell would I know. He knocks me about, beats me, kicks me . . . once he pulled my hair and knocked my head on the floor." Her face turned unhappy, almost pained, and Harjunpaa expected her to burst into tears. But instead she laughed bitterly and hoisted up her skirt.

"Look at these bruises," she shrilled. "They come from kicks."

Harjunpaa took in the whiteness of the thigh, some dark patches, a bit of shiny knickers, lace.

"Take it easy, I'm not a doctor, you know."

His fingers fumbled round the bottom button of his jacket.

She let her skirt fall and grabbed a handbag from the table. Her expression changed again; now it was jubilant, almost vicious. And again she laughed—but this time deep down in her throat.

"So you see, sonny, I'm not an old hag yet, I still have my chances. As long as you catch that shitbag. You can do

135

whatever you want, as long as you catch him, you can stay here and wait, anything."

A few steps and she was in the hall. Harjunpaa tried to stop her.

"Just a moment, Mrs. Melin."

"Bye-bye, sonny."

The door slammed in his face. Harjunpaa reached for the knob but didn't turn it. He could hear her steps clattering down the stairs.

Harjunpaa narrowed his eyes. They couldn't have asked for a better chance to lie in wait. He walked back to the sitting room, took the walkie-talkie out, turned the power up.

"Monica, can you hear Timo?"

"I can hear you. I've tried to call you twice already. The others have just arrived."

"OK. . . . I'm in the flat, alone. In a minute a red-haired, fairly drunk woman will come out. That's Leo's mother. Ask Harko to follow her and check whom she meets—and to let us know when she's on her way back. You stay where you are but ask Wallender to come up.

"All right," Monica spoke slowly. "Didn't the mother know where her son was?"

"No. But it seems he comes here at night, to get food and stuff. I'll tell you more later."

Harjunpaa went into Leo's room. There was a bed, a table full of junk, one light, and a huge, badly worn easy chair. The closet door was open—it seemed some frantic search had taken place; a shirt and a pair of blue cords were hanging half out. On the floor were a few empty beer bottles and some spare parts for a moped. The walls were decorated with a picture of a naked woman and some obscure pop group. A scrawl, made with a thick felt-tip pen applied directly to the wall, declared: HOME SWEET HOME SHIT. It was signed "Sid."

20

Monica was leaning against the building, buttressing herself against the hard wall with her hands. The concrete was rough and dug into her palms. She changed her position and looked at her watch at the same time. Five past midnight already—although it did seem later still. She looked up, no stars or moon were visible, only dark clouds; in the south the darkness was streaked with blue light every now and then. She couldn't hear the thunder, but there were ominous bursts of wind that shook the trees.

From time to time people entered the building she was looking at—there were several staircases—but none of them had alerted her. She had looked at Leo Melin's photograph only briefly, but long enough to remember well his elongated face, and even more important from this distance, she remembered clearly the outline of his thin, drooping shoulders.

A moped approached from the direction of the footpath that led to the playground and the pond. It crossed the front of the house and turned into the car park. Monica looked up sharply, following the moped with her eyes and by the sound. The moped circled around the car park, stopped for a while, and then returned. Monica pushed herself off the wall and bent down to see better between the small trees.

The moped's engine idled. The lights had been switched off. The rider let his feet drag on the ground.

137

Then he stopped altogether, holding onto the metal frame that supported the clotheslines. Monica's breathing was shallow. The rider was a tall, thin boy—he kept looking around and finally stared up at the building, as if to identify a particular window among the hundreds. He made a move to get off, then sat back again—but Monica had seen enough. She unzipped her bag and pulled out her walkie-talkie. The red light came on as soon as she pressed the button.

"Can Timo hear Monica?"

"I hear you."

"Leo's down here. He's on a moped, about thirty yards from the staircase door, can't make his mind up—it seems to me he smells a rat and might make off any minute."

"Has he seen you?"

"I shouldn't think so. But he did go to the car park. I'm sure he knew there were police cars in there."

"Let me know the moment he's on his way in. I'll come down. Wallender can stay here. And Monica, if you can, try to get closer to the car in case he clears off. Keep us posted."

"I will."

"And don't try any tricks on your own."

"Unless I have to."

Monica bit her lip. She was aggrieved that there wasn't much she could do on her own—the distance was too far, about fifty yards. Leo had a moped, she was on foot. But there were trees between them; she believed that Leo wouldn't notice anything as long as she moved in shadow. Monica took a deep breath and straightened up. She moved quickly toward the end of the house, thinking that once she was out of the shadows she'd have to walk normally, so as not to draw attention to herself.

Harjunpaa opened the flat door.

"Shouldn't we both wait here a bit longer?" Wallender's

138

voice was calm somewhere in the darkness of the small hall. "Maybe Monica was wrong, he may well come up in time."

"No." Harjunpaa sounded sharper than he'd intended. He was angry at himself for having sent Harko after Leo's mother instead of telling him to wait with Monica. "Monica's out there alone. And besides, if he was going to come he would be up by now. But be ready to come as soon as we call."

"Sure."

Harjunpaa slipped out and pushed the door closed behind himself. After the darkness of the flat the light coming through the staircase windows was quite adequate to see by. He descended the stairs as fast as he could without making a noise, straining his ears to hear if the door downstairs was opening or if Monica was calling him. He pressed the walkie-talkie to his ear and could feel how the aerial wobbled as he ran, scraping the wall occasionally.

"Timo, this is Monica."

Harjunpaa stopped in his tracks.

"He's going!" Monica shouted. "Some people came and he got the wind up. I tried to stop him, almost got knocked down. He's heading toward the shopping center." Monica was panting, she must have been running. Harjunpaa speeded up, too, he took several stairs at a go, holding onto the handrail, felt it burn his hand. Somewhere above him a door slammed and someone else was running down as well. Wallender must have heard the message. Harjunpaa tried to go faster, he could see trees outside the windows, it couldn't be far to go now.

He rushed out—it was like diving into the outside air, to the smells of the night. Right outside the door was a gang of youngsters, boys and girls; he didn't stop to count them. He ran toward the car park. The youngsters shouted something after him but he didn't listen, his feet were drumming on the tarmac and he was panting. He thought he could see a moped disappear behind the trees. Then the rear lights of the Lada appeared, it was backing toward him, engine revving, Monica waved her hand to hurry him along, Harjunpaa looked behind.

"Wallender," he shouted. "You take the other car! We'll try to catch him!" Then he felt the door handle, tore the door open, and threw himself in.

Monica accelerated and turned the wheel wildly. The car tilted, turned right, its tires scraping the side panels, the mud flaps scraping the ground. Monica changed to third.

"It's only a small moped," she said quietly. "Dark blue. Heading toward the shopping center. He's got no helmet."

Harjunpaa switched the radio on and had the microphone ready. Monica slammed on the brakes, tires screeching. The street ended in a crescent. Toward the left was the shopping center; the only street off, on the right, was straight and empty.

"There he is!" Monica shouted. "He's going down the steps, he's going to ride right through the shopping center."

She changed gear and revved the engine.

"You can't go that way with a car!" Harjunpaa shouted with fright. "We've got to turn around!"

"And let him get away," Monica spat through gritted teeth as she forced the car over the pavement and sped down the grassy slope. Harjunpaa pushed both arms out to brace himself. The steps were on the left. The car listed forward, bushes scraping either side—and then the Lada was horizontal again, rolling down the tarmac of the car park, and then they sped past the telephone kiosk and the taxi rank.

Monica took a sharp turn to the left, toward the end of the shopping center; they reached the covered area, then passed the first building, turned left again—now they

140

were facing the shopping mall that ran the length of the center. Monica dipped the lights and pressed her foot down.

"Wallender, can you hear Harjunpaa calling?" he was panting into the microphone.

"I can hear you. I'm coming down Kotikonnuntie, which way's he going?"

"I'm not sure yet. He went right through the shopping center—he might be trying to get to the pedestrian way that leads to the sports field. Try to get to, say, Tanhuantie, and cut across his path!"

Shop windows and neon lights whisked past. Monica hooted the horn, a girl and a boy jumped to the grass, entwined; somebody was shaking a fist at them, a drunkenly swaying man lurched toward the car and opened his mouth in a shout. Harjunpaa had clenched his teeth; he expected any minute to hear the sides hit the wall with a screech.

"Hold on!" Monica ordered. "We're turning right."

Her voice neared falsetto, and her face was strange, tight, so full of concentration it scared him. She stepped on the brake and changed to a lower gear, bringing the front of the car down—while at the same time swerving the wheel right. She was thrown against Harjunpaa, fair hair whipped across his face, and he had time to think this was Monica's smell before they were back on straight tarmac. The lane opened ahead of them, long and downward-sloping, empty as far as the eye could see, but at the very edge of the light from their headlamps something reflected the light back, a red spot.

"There he goes!"

Trees and bushes became a dark ribbon, whizzing past on either side of the car. Harjunpaa swallowed hard to steady his voice before pressing the button.

"Central. 8-2-5 calling!"

"Go on."

"We're after a boy who slipped from us in Kontula. He's riding a dark blue lightweight moped down the pedestrian lane toward the sports field. He's tall, thin, sixteen years old, called Leo Melin. Can be dangerous. We want him as a suspect for two murders. Norri's back in the office and can give more details in case you need any. Will you put out an alarm."

"Over and out, 8-2-5. Here is a message to all cars out in Kontula or thereabouts—"

Harjunpaa thought that he could detect a bluish band of exhaust in the headlights, coming from the escaping two-stroke engine; he thought he could even smell it, it reminded him of the smell of his own Wartburg. He thought about the boy riding the moped—his hands on the handlebars, turning for more speed, turning for gears; air whizzing past his ears and watering his eyes. And in the back of his mind there would be fear that pushed him on, urged him to go faster and faster on his lightweight moped. And only two days ago he had been quite different, holding that gray piece of rock that now waited in the police garage, waited in the same condition as it was found, as heavy as it was then.

The tarmac ended. Their car met the sandy field with a thump, grit rattled against the underside. To the right they could see streetlights and a building that looked like a school, to the left the wide dark field opened. Monica slowed down. Harjunpaa leaned forward until his face touched the windshield.

"I can see his tracks! Straight on. He's been going at such a lick it's kicked up the sand."

Monica accelerated but stepped on the brake almost at once. They had come to the other side of the field. In front of them was a low hut and a grassy hillside, bushes, trunks of birch trees that glowed white in the headlights. Monica pulled the handbrake on; Harjunpaa jumped out.

He spotted the moped at once. It was lying on its side, its front wheel in the air. In a stride he was there, touching the engine, nearly burning his fingers. He stood up and did some quick thinking. It was hard to run in a wood in the dark, he knew from experience—the boy might well be only a few yards away, lying low under some bushes, waiting for them to go away. It would be best to use dogs—but there was no guarantee that a dog patrol would be available that night, and in any case, by the time the patrol could arrive Leo would have got too much headway—if he had decided to make a run for it. Harjunpaa returned quickly to the car.

Monica was leaning her head on the neck rest, her hands limply in her lap; her face was pale and she was breathing through her mouth, her chest heaving. Harjunpaa grabbed the portable searchlight.

"Monica, that was a damn good chase—you better ask to be transferred permanently to our section once we've got this one cleared up. . . . But now could you let Wallender know where we are—I think he should go to the other side of these woods. And explain the situation to Central and ask for dogs. And could you turn the car so that the lights cover the edge of the trees as far as possible. You can take the other lamp and check the edge of the field on the other side. But don't go in. Stay in the open. And if we do get the dogs will you make sure they don't send them in before I've come out. I'm just checking nearby, not going in far."

"Timo."

"Yes?"

"Nothing, we'll do as you say."

"OK."

Where the moped lay discarded, the grass reached halfway up to his knees. Harjunpaa stood still for a few seconds and stared at the line of trampled grass that led into the woods. Then he pulled his jacket aside, put his hand on his gun, and drew it out: It was dark and heavy, the barrel pointing downward. He took a deep breath and started to follow the track—dry grass rustled around his feet and his shadow moved dark and long from tree to tree.

About twenty yards on, a narrow, partly cobbled track ran parallel to the field. Harjunpaa hesitated, didn't know which way to go. Then he noticed a stand of raspberry canes on the opposite side of the road—the signs of Leo's escape were even clearer here than in the grass: All the broken canes displayed the pale undersides of the leaves. The land sloped upward behind the raspberries—and from that direction came a rattling noise, like pebbles rolling down the exposed hillside. Harjunpaa had bent down and was approaching the bushes when he heard the car behind him in the field—Monica was turning it round and for a moment the whole forest was dipped into total darkness. Harjunpaa switched on his own searchlight. After the car lights its beam seemed red and pale.

In a minute he was on a steep hillside. Through it ran an old digging, maybe it was a trench once. He stopped and swept the area with his lamp—the trench continued on either side as far as he could see. The bottom was filled with rubbish of all sorts: There were even whole bushes, pulled up with their roots, as if someone had been clearing the undergrowth; somewhere beneath the twigs he could hear some small animal scuttling away. He was sure that nobody could move in the bottom of that trench without making a noise that could be heard a good distance away. He listened a moment longer. Far away to his left he could hear a dog barking; from the direction of the city came the sound of sirens; a sudden gust of wind made the trees and bushes rustle. Harjunpaa swung his light toward the trench and jumped over.

Soon he had reached a flat and nearly treeless cliff top.

It wasn't so dark up there, the clouds were a shade lighter, barely a mile away was a well-lit cluster of small detached houses. Harjunpaa had a feeling of unease; he could have sworn that someone was watching him; he switched off his light and crouched, listening. Wind shook the trees down the slope, but around him all was still—there were no sounds to betray movement and nothing else, only his pulse and his watch, but he could feel how shifty and anxious eyes kept a watch on him behind some solitary tree or boulder.

Harjunpaa's grip tightened on his gun—it was wet from his sweaty palm. On a reflex he shifted his thumb to the trigger, cleared his throat.

"Come out, Leo!" he shouted. "I can see you!"

Still keeping low, he moved sideways for a few yards, switched his light on, and waved its beam from side to side. All it uncovered were boulders and iron bars hammered into the rock. He stood up. Next to him was a sandy track. It was full of marks from bicycles and mopeds, but on the top of these he could detect footprints left recently by running feet. Harjunpaa squatted—at places he thought he could recognize an all too familiar pattern. He followed it for about thirty yards. The plateau ended in a steep slope; the track ran out near the edge of the smooth rock. A decayed concrete pipe, almost like a chimney, protruded from the rock. Harjunpaa did not stop to wonder what its function was. He ran to the cliff edge and shone his lamp down: The drop was some three yards, maybe more—but nearby the rock sloped downward at irregular angles, like huge steps. Thousands of feet must have gone down that way; there was no moss or grass on the steps. He crouched, dropped to the nearest step, walked to the edge, and jumped to the next step.

Harjunpaa turned his lamp off when he reached the bottom. He stood still by the rockface—it went up behind him like a wall, blocking out all light. It also blocked all sounds of traffic or habitation—he could have been in the middle of a huge forest, miles from anywhere. The air was moist, smelling of moss and barely noticeably of rusted iron and of rocks sweating in the perpetual darkness underground.

Harjunpaa switched his light back on. Broken glass and signs of old camp fires covered the ground. He walked further a little way, taking care not to tread on glass. This side of the rockface was hacked flat. It ended in a dark opening, barely high enough for a man standing upright and only a little wider. It was framed with iron, now black with rust; thick hinge stubs remained on one side. Harjunpaa advanced slowly, then stopped. He seemed to remember that during the First World War part of Helsinki's fortifications had been a chain of tunnels, most of which had since been blocked up. This one must have been one of those which for some reason was never filled up.

Harjunpaa crept forward, but a few yards before reaching the opening he stopped again; he felt an unreasonable revulsion at the thought of entering the tunnel, a feeling that was linked with many irrational fears of childhood: He half-expected that something slimy would drop down on his neck from the ceiling, or that a hand, green with moss, would reach for him from some cranny. His reason told him all this was rubbish, that the tunnel was empty of horrors and that he had to check it because it was an ideal hiding place. But again he had this sensation of being watched.

"To hell with it."

Harjunpaa moved his finger on the trigger, took a firmer grip on the lamp, hunched his shoulders, and stepped in. He came into a concrete lobby, its floor littered with rubbish—Christmas trees of bygone years, the white shell of a washing machine, a gumboot, a skeleton

146

of a car seat; all hampered his advance. In addition he could hear water slopping under his feet at every step. The smell of being under ground grew stronger. Water was dripping somewhere, quietly, persistently.

There was another opening, leading on from the lobby. That was where the tunnel proper started, at an almost ninety-degree angle to his left. Harjunpaa looked in. The darkness was so intense it sucked his light in. All he could discern were some naked rock walls, nothing at all of the floor—it was under brown water. Through the water gleamed an old tin bucket without a handle. Here the water was half a yard deep; further on, the bottom seemed to run deeper.

Harjunpaa strained his ears. His own breathing bounced back at him. There was the sound of dripping water and some other sounds, so distant they were barely audible—the tunnel had to be tens of yards long. You couldn't go in without a boat of some sort. Harjunpaa sighed with relief, turned round, and hurried out. He didn't climb back to the top of the cliff but skirted around the rock instead. In a few minutes he burst through the shrubbery, out onto the sports field. A few hundred feet away were the lights of the Lada; still further on was Monica with her lamp.

"Monica," Harjunpaa called. "It's me, Timo!"

Monica stopped and turned to face him. Behind her, on the road leading to the field, the flashing lights of a dog patrol were approaching at high speed.

21

Mikael huddled in the tent surrounded by darkness. He could no longer tell whether his eyes were open or closed—either way it was as dark—but he thought they were open, for had they been closed he was sure he would again see that man lying on the ground—and see his head as it had been when Leo lifted the stone up for the second time.

Mikael shrank within himself. Now that he had both of the blankets it wasn't so shiveringly cold. It wasn't so damp, either—he and Leo had gone to the opposite end of the cave and pushed stakes up the hole that led to the top of the cliff. The hole was too narrow for them to crawl through, but at least it let more air in now. The air had become drier and the smoke disappeared more quickly; in the daytime a gray streak of light penetrated the hole.

Now he could hear sounds again.

The sounds made him feel as if something cold and sharp and hard churned inside his belly. His body became rigid.

Apart from the darkness, the sounds were the worst thing to endure when Leo was away. It was the echo that made them so horrible—you could never tell whether they were near or far away, nor could you tell if it was Leo on his way back or somebody else. There were sounds of dripping water. If you started to listen you'd

148

begin to believe that someone was running on the water, or that some large animal was smacking its lips.

Mikael pulled the blanket down and raised his head. He thought he could hear rhythmic splashing and rippling from the tunnel. He sat up and fumbled for the torch, crept to the flap, and lifted it up. The darkness didn't diminish. He wanted to flash the torch, although Leo had told him not to; even only once, very quickly. He pressed the switch. The light seemed incredibly bright. Mikael had to blink his eyes—only then could he see the rough rock ceiling and the piece of level rock, barely the size of his room at home, on which the tent stood. Water lapped against the edge of the rock near the tent. He had time to see the remnants of their campfire and the pine twigs ready for burning before the light went out, just as before: Suddenly it turned red and then there was nothing left of it but the glowing filaments under the glass.

Then he heard the whistle—it was short and hissing, done with teeth; it had to be Leo, no one else could whistle like that. Mikael crept out of the tent and jumped up. He was so relieved that he trembled; he had this constant fear that Leo would be caught or that he would just go away and leave him behind. And now he could see light! It came along the water like a string of pearls and revealed where the cave ended and the tunnel proper began. Mikael crouched, stood up, he didn't know which way to be. Leo was near the corner now, ripples in the water grew larger, there was a grunt—and now a clatter when the stake they used to push the raft hit the wall.

"Leo!" Mikael shouted. Echo took the word from his mouth and multiplied it. Leo said something indistinct, then he rounded the corner and the light was so bright Mikael had to shade his eyes. Leo adjusted the torch so that it hit the water and the raft, no larger than a desk. The raft had been put together from blocks of styrofoam

149

and empty plastic containers, and tied together with metal wire. It could easily carry one person but with two on board you had to stand absolutely still, and even so water came up to your shoes.

"Leo! Shit, you don't know how I've waited."

"Shut up! Shut your mouth, you bloody fool!"

"Sid."

Mikael's mouth dropped open. He could sense rather than see that Leo was nervous—so scared that even his voice was strange. Mikael bent down and held the raft with stiff hands, then pulled it halfway up the rock. Leo jumped off without a word. His jogging shoes were squelching, they dripped with water. And his jeans were dark and plastered to his legs—water ran in rivulets from the bottoms.

Leo took one quick step, then another, but didn't know which way to go—the torch in his hand wavered, shooting its beam to the tent and rock and water in turn.

"Bloody, fucking, shit hell."

Mikael crouched quietly; he didn't dare ask anything. Bewildered, his eyes followed Leo as he snatched some twigs and rammed them between the stones that ringed the fireplace. He searched for matches, lit one—shivering all the time with cold, shivering so hard his face trembled and his lips were pulled back into a snarl. The dry twigs caught fire easily. Soon the whole cave was filled with red light and restlessly flickering shadows. Only then Mikael realized that Leo had come back empty-handed, had brought no food or clothes, nothing. Leo slumped down without even pulling his wet trousers off. Then he said quietly: "Those shitbags got my moped."

Mikael crept closer. Leo rested his chin on his knees. He stared at the fire and the flames reflected in his eyes, making them seem brimful of blood.

"I knew at once that something wasn't right," he said. "In our car park there was a Lada that looked just like a

150

pigcart. And there was another one at the next car park. And when I was right outside our house I got a horrible feeling. And then when I cleared off, some cow tried to stop me. They came after me. I bet they were pigs from SUOPO. They must have been hanging round in there, waiting for me. . . . I went right through the center and they came after me, but didn't dare come down the steps. I left my moped down by that hut and ran up to the cliff—I saw them going over it, I bet they took it away. . . . I was flat on my belly on the cliff top and one pig came after me there. I could've dropped him there if I had had something on me. Then he followed me but I didn't wait."

"They know it was us."

"I couldn't use the stake because it's so slow. I went into the water and pushed the raft. I just made it to that first hole before the pig got to the tunnel. I saw his light. He poked his head in. But I bet the water was just too much for him."

"I heard voices before you got in. They know that it's us."

"Hell, I was like some bloody duck. Sat in that hole and didn't make a sound while that pig was there. I bet he was waiting just outside. I was there at least fifty hours. And then I heard them again. At least two of them, there was. And I heard whining, like they had dogs. They brought the dogs after me like we was some bloody criminals. Those pigs were trying to push the dogs in but they didn't go. I could hear how the dog strained, you know like when it pulls so it can't breathe and whines. It was whining and pulling and then they took it away. I didn't move, I waited. Didn't come until now."

Leo stood up stiffly and started to peel his trousers off with trembling hands. Mikael swallowed so hard it made a noise. His stomach was hurting and he felt the same way he did when he closed his eyes and saw those things.

"I guess we killed him," Mikael said with difficulty. "And they know it was us."

"Sure, sure, no doubt there. I bet it's my mother, she's a bitch. I bet she's been telling them tales—and the pigs have guessed the rest. Or else somebody saw us. Could've been that cow who was drawing the curtains in that window."

"We killed him."

Leo squeezed water from his trousers, flapped them irritably in the air.

"What are you going on about? You should've thought about that before. You wasn't told to kill anybody."

Mikael stood up and stepped closer to Leo. His hands twitched and he opened his mouth anxiously a couple of times before he was able to say, "How do you mean I killed him? Why d'you say that? It was you who took the stone."

"So what? You was there all the time. Sure you knew what was what. I thought he would snuff it. But I thought why not—better put him out of his misery. His face was so smashed up anyway that they couldn't have done anything with it. Anyway, who cares, one creep less. When you look around every place is full of creeps like that, so many creeps around you can't breathe for the stink. Besides, after that stone, you still kicked him."

"I couldn't stop. Somehow . . . I just couldn't. All the time I thought that he was our Sod. And I thought of Jani. I couldn't stop."

"Well then, don't bloody well go on about it."

Leo threw his trousers down by the fire. Then he crept into the tent, flipping the blankets about as he searched for a comfortable position.

Mikael fell slowly down to his knees. He couldn't think clearly, his brain kept repeating that he had killed a man. The thought no longer gave him pain, he didn't even feel guilt—nothing. There was just this fact, running in meaningless repetition in his mind: He had killed a man. Slowly he ceased to mind what would happen to him—he knew he wouldn't have cared even if his father had rounded the corner with other police right then; all he could handle was being there in the cave, all he could take in was the smell of rock and water and smoke, the play of shadows on the walls, and the sound of water, like a huge animal smacking its lips.

"That female pig who was trying to stop me—she should have come after me," said Leo in the tent. "I'd have got her. She'd keep me warm now, she's got big tits. Tomorrow we'll go and dry my clothes up on the top. Better leave it till the afternoon, though. And then we'll clear out of here. We'll pick up some new clothes and some money in town. We can go to my father in Sweden, he'll know what we should do."

Mikael didn't respond. He was counting the drops of water, mesmerized.

"Did you hear me, Miku?"

"Your father is there in prison," he said in a low voice. "You told me yourself."

There was annoyed tossing about in the tent. Then Leo shouted, "You spoil everything! You don't have to tell me he's in the clink, just as if I didn't know! You're just like all the rest, a real dumb one! You don't want me to have anything since you think I'm a shit and my mother's a whore."

Mikael thought how odd it was that once men had excavated this tunnel for some specific reason that no longer existed; the only use the tunnel and the cave had now was for them to hide in it, as if they no longer existed, either.

"I'm quitting this place," Mikael said after many minutes had passed.

"So am I," Leo answered from the tent, from underneath the blankets. "We'll quit together tomorrow."

"I mean I'm going now, tonight."

Leo was silent, then he tried to laugh. In the end he asked: "And where d'you think you're going?"

"Home."

Leo laughed derisively for a long time. Then he said in a nasty tone, "Must I tell you what your dad will do to you, and that's nothing to what they'll do to you at the station. They'll rip your pants off and they'll make you put your balls on the table and then they'll give you a lesson or two with the old truncheon."

Leo was agitated. His voice was louder now, he must be sitting up.

"And then when you say you're thirsty they'll tell you to drink your piss. In the end you will."

"I don't care," Mikael whispered. Leo was silent for a long while, then he said, somewhat anxiously: "You can't go. You can't leave me when we've been together all this time. I was mates with Jani, too. You can't."

"I can't stand this place."

"But *I'm* with you, *I'm* not afraid. It's nothing to me, it's like it's always been, I've always felt like I was in a cave or something. And I don't think it will make any difference if we quit, it'll still feel the same way. Everybody hates me because I'm like this—they know they'll get old and drop off but I'll carry on the same way. So they never give me a chance. And I hate them all and they know it. You can't go."

"I'll go to Ulla."

Leo crawled to the flap on all fours and ripped the flap aside.

"You do that," he shouted roughly. "I know what she is. She's a whore! You think she'll let you? You go there and I'll follow you and I'll do to her what I did to that man. You won't want to fuck her once her head's like a pancake!"

154

Leo closed the flap again and burrowed back into the blankets; it sounded as if he was sobbing.

Mikael was still on his knees. He cried silently but so desperately that his knees got wet with dripping tears.

Some twenty minutes later Leo crawled out of the tent.

"You know what, Miku?" he said and from his voice you could tell he wanted to be mates again.

"We'll break into your place. We can get in through the window of that room downstairs. And we can bring all your father's guns over here. And every time a copper pushes his head around the corner we'll blast him—the water will splash when they drop in, one after the other. And in the end they'll give up and say that we can fly to any country we want, so long as we don't shoot no more. And you can ask Ulla to come with you. How's that? Shall we go now?"

22

"Put it down! Timo—my fingers."

Harko loosened his grip and the front of the boat fell down. Harjunpaa, who was holding the back, took one step too many and hit his knee on the edge.

"Damn."

He let the back go and it hit the mossy ground with a thump. There it lay, the boat, a splash of orange in the broken twigs in the wood.

It wasn't noon yet but the day was already hot. But it was a different heat from the previous days. During the night there had been a huge downpour and now the air shimmered with humidity. Clothes felt tacky, as if they had been in a room full of steam; and the smell of moist lichen and moss was strong. Harjunpaa wiped his forehead and avoided looking at the boat, which seemed to declaim that they were about to do something idiotic and that it was all his fault.

"Are you quite sure you didn't hop all over the place and mess up the tracks?" the dog handler had asked him the previous night.

"I just had a look around the edge of the woods on this side," said Harjunpaa. The dog handler had looked at him for a while, his head to one side. Then he said something to his mate and to his dog and disappeared with them through the raspberry canes. Less than ten minutes later they had reappeared on the sports field, at exactly the same spot as Harjunpaa himself had done a little earlier. The Alsatian had stopped at Harjunpaa's feet, sniffing them eagerly.

"I see," the dog handler had grunted. "You went through those raspberries and jumped over the old trench. Then you spent some time on the cliff top and followed a footpath. Then you went down the side of the rocks, visited the entrance to the tunnel, looked in, and then ran back around that way. In other words, you had a look at the edge of the woods on this side . . . yes."

On the second go the dog again simply followed the tracks left by Harjunpaa. On the third go the handler had skirted the whole little forest, hoping to find any tracks leading out. Either there were no such tracks or else the traffic on the road had wiped them out. No results had been achieved by a search in the woods, lasting an hour and a half.

Now it was Thursday and Harjunpaa and Harko were standing among the trees, their arms numb from carting the boat from the road. All because they had discovered that the water in the bottom of the tunnel reached up to their waists, and since Norri had decided, having assessed the situation, that they should go in.

"We must check that place. Especially in the light of what Mrs. Melin said Leo had taken from home. Besides, that's the only hiding place around here where he could have bolted to so quickly. No, it's got to be done."

Harjunpaa looked back the way they had come. The road was over 200 yards away, barely visible from here; only a corner of the police van and trailer parked on the verge could still be seen behind the bushes. Then he looked ahead, estimating the distance they still had to cover—barely 40 yards to go. The rock face was there, behind some sparse spruces, rising up like a wall. He could see the steplike formation well in the corner; near there was the mouth of the tunnel. A thrush was twittering somewhere nearby.

157

"Shall we go in?" Harjunpaa grabbed the back of the boat again. "We're nearly there."

Together they lifted the boat and, grunting and panting, they dragged it uphill through the woods; the searchlights banged against its sides, and twigs and branches broke under their Wellingtons, while the insides of the same boots broke the skin of their heels. The only consolation Harjunpaa could imagine was not having tried to approach the tunnel from the sports field—the retinue of jeering kids they would have attracted would have been too much to bear.

In the long shadow thrown by the rock, the air was instantly cooler. The smells changed, too; now it was damp rock and rotting concrete, water lapping darkly at the heart of the rock. There was some other smell, too, less easy to define; it stirred feelings at the back of your mind, long since forgotten, still and ever so slightly threatening. Sounds changed as well; it became quieter, a perpetual nighttime seemed to radiate from the rock.

"We better take it right to the opening."

When they put the boat down, both were panting for air. There was far more litter than Harjunpaa had noticed on the previous night—tires and canisters, beer cans, the skeleton of a moped, red with rust; it seemed that the people who had dumped their rubbish here had not wanted to go into the tunnel. Initials and other graffiti, now weathered away, had been painted on the rock face. But the mouth of the tunnel was as he remembered it: black and still.

"A somewhat grim place. Hard to believe anyone would choose to stay in there."

"Let's see how can we get the boat in," Harjunpaa said as he stepped into the anteroom, finding his way amongst the rubbish. The air was much cooler in here, his skin felt the chill, he was almost cold. He switched his light on and aimed the beam at the tunnel. The white beam was

sucked away in ten yards. He aimed the light at the walls:
Each rough edge and bump threw dark shadows. He
turned his light at the ceiling and instinctively
crouched—the whole ceiling was alive with fluttering. He
had to stare at it for a while before he understood what it
was: The ceiling was full of butterflies, large and quite
dark when their wings were closed, but when the light hit
them their wings opened and shone red.

"Harko. Come and look at this."

Harko had not moved from the outer opening. He
stood stiffly, holding the rusty door frame with one hand.
Since the light was behind Harko, Harjunpaa couldn't see
his face. But he realized all was not well and made his
way back to the doorway. Harko retreated from the
opening, his face white; even his lips had lost all color.
Shiny little beads had appeared on his forehead.

"Timo," he said in a low voice, avoiding Harjunpaa's
eyes, as if ashamed. "I can't . . . you remember that
Saseka case . . . I realized at the door that I can't."

Harjunpaa stood still. Then he remembered: In April
a workman had decided to kill himself by jumping down
from a disused factory chimney, lost his balance in the
wind and fell inward, down the pipe, instead. He had
died instantly as he hit the rubbish at the bottom. Harko
had been on duty that night. He had crawled along a
channel barely big enough for a man until he reached the
bottom of the chimney. Then he straightened the dead
man's limbs as best he could so that he could pull the
body back with him. But crawling backward in the dark
he had taken a wrong turn and ended at a locked steel
shutter. The shutter closed his way out, the corpse
blocked his way back. It was an hour before the men waiting outside realized that something had gone wrong.

"OK." Harjunpaa spoke slowly. He didn't want to enter
the tunnel on his own—and besides, he couldn't row and
handle the lamps at the same time. And what could he do

if he did actually find someone inside, let alone if both the boys they were looking for were hiding in there. Monica and Wallender were posted some miles away. Harjunpaa said in a matter-of-fact way: "We'll contact Monica and Wallender, I bet they're bored stiff by now and ready for anything. You change places with one of them, I don't mind. You know nothing could make me climb a roof."

"OK. Thanks, Timo." Harko took his jacket from the boat and half ran toward the van.

Harjunpaa lit a cigarette and went back in. After a score of telephone calls that morning he had got hold of an army captain who told him that the tunnel could be 100 to 200 yards long—it had been excavated shortly before the First World War, and there were some ten like this one around Helsinki; the captain had never heard that any plans or drawings of the tunnel existed. Harjunpaa stood still: Drops hit water, one after another, as they had done close to a hundred years. There were no other sounds, nothing to hint that somebody was hiding in the tunnel. He threw his cigarette into the water, where it went out with a hiss. Then he cleared his throat with determination, went out, took hold of the boat, and began to drag it in over the rubbish.

Some twenty minutes later the boat was bobbing on the water. Harjunpaa stood next to it, holding it by the side. Water came almost to the top of his boots and it was chillingly cold; his feet felt frozen already.

"Climb in," he shouted to Monica, "since you wanted to come boating."

Harko's boots were too big for Monica; they came almost to her knees. She gathered her wide skirt into a bundle round her thighs, clambered over the side, and sat at the back. Her skin was very pale; she'd had no time all that summer to get a tan. Harjunpaa climbed to the front and fitted the oars; secretly he was glad Monica had

160

come and not Wallender. Even the air had a different feel to it now, softer and warmer—it smelt of Monica; the tunnel was no longer quite so gloomy.

Harjunpaa pulled on the oars and let the boat glide. It quickly grew darker; the darkness closed in around them, became a substance through which they were moving— the mouth of the tunnel was but a gray slit. The echoes multiplied every sound; if another boat had been coming they wouldn't have heard it in time. Harjunpaa disliked sitting with his back to the direction he was going—he had to look over his shoulder all the time to keep the boat from hitting the wall—and he disliked it for other reasons as well.

Monica cast the beam down and bent forward.

"Timo," she whispered. "If you think about it, the water's so cold no one could swim in it. What I mean is, if somebody's in there he'd have to have a boat or a raft or something."

They stared at each other. There were sharp shadows on Monica's face. Harjunpaa recalled that they'd seen nothing suitable to use as a raft so far; if one was used in the tunnel it had to be somewhere inside.

"That's true."

He was whispering, too.

They were silent for a moment, then Harjunpaa whispered: "I'll turn the other way. You keep the light on the left wall, I'll keep mine on the right side. And Monica . . . you'd better be ready for anything."

He detached the oars, took one of them as a paddle, and knelt in the bow, facing the way they were going. From the corner of his eye he could see Monica had understood his meaning—she had taken her bag and opened it; she was holding the butt of her revolver: Next to the shiny gun her hand seemed very small and pale.

Harjunpaa used the paddle on either side in turn; the paddle cut through the beam of light rhythmically and its

161

shadow jumped on the walls like some escaping animal. Drops of water falling on their head were freezing cold now. Harjunpaa's hands were cold, yet he was sweating. Again he let the boat glide. There was something dark on the lefthand side. Harjunpaa put the paddle down across the bow, took his light and switched it on, sweeping the darkness with its beam. The boat floated to the right and scraped against the wall.

The tunnel divided into two.

What he had seen was the opening of another tunnel, nothing more sinister. He rested for a while, leaning on his paddle, getting his breathing steady.

"Bloody hell."

He gave the boat a shove by pushing it away from the wall and it glided closer to this new tunnel. It was not very large, maybe three yards wide and five yards deep; at the very end the rock formed a shelf a yard or so above the water. That shelf was empty but at one end there was a darker patch, all that was left of a campfire, burnt out long since.

"Oh," Monica sighed. "I thought that something would jump on us from there . . . something . . ."

Harjunpaa said nothing; his lips felt tight and dry, his heart was still thumping.

"This boat's like a peapod," Monica whispered before Harjunpaa had resumed his paddling. "Have you thought what we'll do if we find someone and he won't come nicely?"

Harjunpaa stared straight ahead. A moment ago he had wondered whether they could swim back if there was a skirmish and the boat capsized. He licked his lips uncertainly. They could turn back and get more help. But what use would that be? The boat couldn't carry many more people. And somebody had to go all the way in—and they had come quite a way already. Besides, he could imagine how Wallender would smile in that smug, self-confident way he had and say, "Well, let's get back to that boat, then."

Harjunpaa turned.

"Monica, if you think it's better . . ."

Monica had stretched her neck and was sniffing the air; Harjunpaa could feel goose pimples popping up on his arms.

"Can you smell it?"

Harjunpaa sniffed with wide nostrils.

"Smoke?"

"Yes," Monica whispered. "And it's no old smoke from the walls, it's fresh. It's so fresh that there has to be a fire somewhere in here right now."

Harjunpaa slipped his hand over his belt and pushed open the press button on the gun shield. He lowered the gun to the bow between his knees.

"Do you remember last night when we were combing the woods," he said in a hoarse whisper. "The dog handler thought once or twice that he could smell smoke. Only he thought it came from that group of houses. There has to be a ventilation pipe from the tunnel up to the cliff."

"What should we do, Timo?"

Harjunpaa was silent for a long while. Monica's face was tense but her eyes were steady; her breathing was fast. Harjunpaa turned to her, bending closer.

"I think we should go and see who it is," he said in a whisper.

"OK." Monica sighed, then her skirt rustled and Harjunpaa could feel her fingers around his wrist, squeezing hard.

"I'm a bit afraid."

"So am I," Harjunpaa confessed hoarsely. "Would you rather—"

"No. I'd never hear the end of it—especially since

163

I'm not a man. We'll go and take a look, OK?" She let go of his wrist and moved back to her seat.

Harjunpaa stood quietly for a while; something had been at the back of his mind for a while, he hadn't wanted to mention it, hadn't wanted to scare Monica, but now he felt he had to, he had no choice, he couldn't possibly take a risk that might be too big for him to bear.

"Monica, we're sailing in what is like a lighthouse. And we've no idea whether they have guns."

Monica shifted, was silent. Then she whispered: "Leo's info has no mention of him ever having carried guns. Once he was found with a knife, but even then he hadn't used it. And he is only sixteen; the other boy is probably even younger."

"We could keep a watch on the tunnel, outside."

"That could take days. And what if there's another way out? I don't think we've any choice, we must go and see."

"Then we go. But just in case, hold the lamp outside the boat, with your arm stretched out."

He turned round, took his paddle, pushed the boat forward.

Sweat glued his shirt to his back; something dropped from the ceiling and slid slowly down his forehead. Uneasily he thought he had made an unsound decision. He tried to convince himself that Leo couldn't possibly know who was coming, he wouldn't start shooting blindly—but then he remembered Taisto Nilsson and Orvo Lagman and he wasn't quite so sure; and although he tried to keep his eyes on the wall where Monica's lamp threw some light, every now and then his eyes slipped toward the darkness into which he was pushing the boat and he found himself thinking what the flash of the gun in front of him would look like and whether there would be time to do anything after seeing it.

The sound of the lapping water changed, there had to be a change of some kind in the tunnel ahead. Harjunpaa

164

lowered the paddle and picked up his lamp; he had lost his sense of distance ages ago—it might well be that they had reached the end of the tunnel by now. The smell of smoke was very strong. But there was no light anywhere. There was another smell, too, vaguely familiar; it took a couple of seconds before Harjunpaa knew what it was: a smell he had known after innumerable fires—the acrid smell of charred wood and ashes recently soaked with water. And then he saw that there was a rough, uneven wall right in front of the boat. They had come to a T-junction; the tunnel continued to either side.

Harjunpaa put his paddle down and crawled cautiously toward the center of the boat. Monica pressed the lamp against her thigh, leaving just enough light for them to see each other's faces. Harjunpaa bent forward. Monica leaned toward him, so close that Harjunpaa felt her hair on his cheek.

"They must have put the fire out very recently," he whispered. "I bet they heard us coming. We are almost in a T-junction. We can get the boat there quietly if I push with my hands, on the wall. Better put the lights out, though. We'll have them ready—and guns, too. We'll switch the lights on together when I give the sign. You'll point yours to the right, I'll point mine to the left. And keep as low as you can. All clear?"

"All clear." The words seemed to come from deep down in her throat.

Harjunpaa reached his hand out and felt the coldness of the rock. He got a good grip on the wall and pushed—the boat moved on so slowly that it made barely any noise at all. Monica switched off her light. Harjunpaa groped his way back to the bow. He held the revolver in his right hand and the lamp in his left, directing both over the edge, toward the darkness. Then he lowered his hand as far down as he could, trying to calculate how far they had come—but seconds and distances were whizzing round his head chaotically.

He sensed rather than knew that they had to be very close to the end wall.

"Now, Monica!"

A beam of light cut through the darkness. The tunnel on his left wasn't very long, maybe some ten yards. In the far end the rock formed a shelf. On the shelf was pitched a green tent, surrounded by stones and bundles of clothes.

"Only a wall on this side," whispered Monica, turning her light to the same direction as Harjunpaa's. Harjunpaa held his breath. A makeshift raft, made of styrofoam and plastic canisters tied together, was pulled halfway up the rock. Water trickled amid the ring of stones around the fireplace. Blue smoke circled high up in the ceiling.

"Come out, Leo!" Harjunpaa shouted. Echo ran the words together and tossed them back in a jumble. Harjunpaa put his thumb on the safety catch and pulled—the click was sharp and metallic.

"Come out, Leo!"

Still no movement from the tent. Harjunpaa looked round the walls; there was no other exit.

"We'll paddle over," he whispered. "You take the other oar. I'll jump on the rock and you'll keep the boat far enough away for them not to jump in. Don't come back until I call. And keep your light fixed on the tent all the time. I'll switch mine off."

He paddled a stroke or two, crouched on the bow, and lifted one leg over the side.

"That's it."

Now he had both feet on the rock, and he held the boat so it couldn't come in any closer. Keeping low, he clambered out and pushed the boat away. He stood still, gripping his gun. Still no sound came from the tent. He knew that Leo could shoot through the canvas—but also

166

that Monica was in greater danger since his light was out and he was standing in the dark. He knew there was no time to lose, and forced himself to move. A pair of wet jeans was spread out next to the extinguished campfire. Another pair was dumped in a bundle nearby—it seemed to Harjunpaa that the jeans had dried into a stiff heap the way clothes saturated with blood usually do.

He stopped at the tent and took a deep breath. Pointing the lamp at the flap he eased it open with the hand gripping the gun. He switched on his light.

In the middle of the tent was a mattress. Someone was huddled on it, wrapped in blankets.

"Get up!" Harjunpaa's voice was gruff. "Up, Leo. This is the police."

The pile of blankets moved. A dirty hand appeared, pushing the covers aside. Harjunpaa recognized Leo at once. But the boy looked different from his photographs—his face was sallow and dirty, it seemed he had been crying; his hair was matted and a tic was pulling one side of his mouth down. The bright light made him blink and press both hands to his face, as if he never wanted to see anything again.

23

"Miku, wake up."

Mikael couldn't remember where he was. He knew he'd have to run at a moment's notice—his legs were moving now as they often did just before sleep.

Then he remembered; something went limp inside him, he gasped for air. He didn't lift his head at once, he wanted to have some more time.

Mikael opened his eyes and looked: a snow white radiator, beneath it a strip of wall, then a skirting board, stained dark. The pillowcase had the smell of fresh linen. He could smell something else as well—coffee and fried eggs, an open window and the day outside: tarmac baking in the sun, and flowers out on the balcony.

And still something else; Mikael closed his eyes again. Ulla had to be somewhere very close by. If he inhaled deeply he could smell her face cream; if he listened he could hear her expectant breathing. Now she knelt down—her skirt rustled softly, joints creaked, bangles clinked against each other. A hand pressed Mikael's naked shoulder, the fingers warm and soft.

"Do get up now. I know you're awake." A hard lump stuck in his throat. Mikael blinked. He had lived this moment a hundred times: Ulla close to him, holding him in her arms, he feeling the softness and the warmth of her skin and the ticklishness of her hair on his face. Mikael spun around. Ulla was there, by his head; she wore a short skirt, her knees were round, her thighs white. Her

168

other hand was in her lap, it pressed her breasts up, he could see the dark circles through her shirt. Her eyes were smiling but the expression on her face reminded Mikael of someone passing a pram on the street, looking. Something hot and suffocating rose up from his belly. Then he realized he was holding tight on Ulla's wrist. He heard his own voice, strange and indistinct: "Come down here."

Ulla was startled. Her eyebrows shot up. But she wasn't scared, she was still smiling, she said in an auntyish voice: "Well, well, so little Mikael wants to be on mummy's lap."

She ruffled his hair and her smell was stronger than before.

"Why don't you . . . be nice to me . . . hold me. Say something nice."

Mikael tugged Ulla by the wrist, hard. He could no longer meet her eye—he was afraid that she would look scornful or ridicule him; he was afraid that she would look embarrassed like his mother when he hugged her. He was already ashamed of what he had said. Yet all he could do was pull harder. Ulla had been balanced on the balls of her feet; now she waved her other hand in the air to regain balance, couldn't, fell on him.

Mikael's fingers groped Ulla's breasts, slid under her arm, around her back, he held her close, with all his might. Ulla's breath was hot on his face, her hair swept over his forehead. Mikael breathed hard, panting.

"Mummy darling. Dearest Ulla."

Ulla got hold of the radiator, pushed, tore herself free. Then she was standing up and pulling her skirt down, wiping hair from her eyes; her face was frightfully sharp and her mouth very narrow.

"You listen to me, Miku." Her voice shook and her breasts went up and down with her breathing. "I'm an adult, I can do what I choose. But you are just a kid, a child. I took you in last night because you were in trouble

169

and needed my help. I thought you were my friend. Don't you start anything. I'm up to here with groping men."

Suddenly she looked almost angry—there were small wrinkles round her nose and her upper lip curled, showing teeth and gum.

"Besides, I'm beginning to think you're a liar as well," she said in a voice that no longer was angry. Then she turned on her heels and walked out of the room, her bare feet sticking to the floor.

Mikael turned to lie on his stomach, and buried his face in the pillow. He pressed his eyes shut so tight that it hurt around the temples, he panted for air with an open mouth; shame overwhelmed him, all else was in abeyance, but ready and waiting to crush down on him like a rock. All he could think about was that he had spoiled it, destroyed the ony thing in his life that had been pleasurable. His fingers gripped the mattress and nothing could stop the tears—they forced their way through his tightly closed lids, soaked into the pillowcase.

The ducks had thought they were in for a treat—they kept coming closer even when the man was already half in the water; when he threw the second or the third stone onto the man's stomach, the biggest one, the one that was almost too heavy to lift—then the man had grunted and bitten his lip and asked: "Are you even human?" But that other man had been smarmy, just the way Sod was when he was trying to get a cheap deal in a shop. He had said again and again: "You can have all I've got, cigs and my money, my watch. Please, stop it, boys, please." Mikael was sobbing, pressing his face so deep into the pillow that only the back of his head could be seen.

"Come and have something to eat."

Mikael lifted his head. Ulla was in the kitchen or in the other room, her voice had been distant and toneless, it was a voice she used to talk to strangers. Mikael wiped his face. When he sat up he felt all his limbs were numb and his mind was the same, lifeless. His clothes were in a pile on the floor, even Leo's jeans that were too long for him. Ulla had dried them and put them there for him. Quietly he got dressed.

He had crossed the living room and was in the doorway to the hall before Ulla saw him.

"Well," she said, "aren't you going to have something to eat before you go? And where do you plan to go, anyway?"

Mikael kept his eyes on the floor. All the same he knew Ulla was standing with her legs apart, hands on her hips, head to one side.

"Home."

"I see, Master Miku thinks that home is good enough for him after all," Ulla said, but it didn't sound as if she was mocking.

"Yes. My father will kill me. But it doesn't matter. I deserve it."

Ulla stiffened. Then she inhaled quickly and took a step closer, grabbed his shoulders, pinching hard.

"Look," she said in an angry voice. "You stop all that constant jabber about killing right now, d'you hear. You killed a man, your father will kill you. . . . Do you know something—a few days ago I saw a man who really *had* been killed . . . he had . . . he was there, in the woods, not far from here, and he had no face left at all. You should have seen that. Then you'd stop talking about killing."

Mikael stood limply, not resisting the shaking Ulla gave him. He didn't open his eyes, he didn't dare; if he had to look at her now he would faint and fall down.

He whispered, "But Sod *will* kill me. And I killed that man. . . ."

"Mikael!" Ulla screamed, shoving him with fury. "Stop it! Don't say it, even as a joke! People who can do something like that, kill like that, they don't have any right to

171

live . . . killers like that only deserve to do the same to themselves."

Mikael slumped against Ulla, who angrily shook herself free. But he had had time to feel how warm and soft she was, how full of life; like those men must have been once. He thought that Ulla must be safe, that no harm must ever come to her, to nobody like Ulla. He turned and went out. When the door closed behind him the sound echoed in the staircase, it was like being back in the tunnel, only now he was no longer afraid.

24

"Find out if you want. It's none of my business, it's your job. . . ."

Harjunpaa turned his eyes from Leo to Norri, who was behind his desk, dressed in a jacket and tie, hands resting on the top of the desk, palms down. But from the way his head was inclined and his gaze occasionally wandered around the room, Harjunpaa knew that Norri was trying to make a difficult decision.

"Let's go back to Monday morning," Norri said in a calm voice. "Why don't you start by telling us what time you woke up and where?"

"You can go back where you want. I'll sit right here. I told you already that there's no point in you telling me I've killed somebody—that's the business of those who snuffed it . . . or you can start beating me up, I bet you know how."

Harjunpaa stole a sideways look at Leo. It was hard to believe that this was the same boy, shivering with fear and cold, whom he had brought out of the tunnel only a few hours ago.

Leo was sitting on a hard plastic chair, quite relaxed, one leg over the other, his elbow over the back of the chair—every now and then he would whistle through his teeth, snapping the fingers of one hand to the beat. He wore dark blue overalls with POLICE SUOPO written across the chest. On his feet he had gray cotton socks and plimsolls with no laces. Losing one's own clothes and having to

173

wear stiff, impersonal overalls sometimes had a depressing effect on the arrested person, but the effect on Leo seemed to be quite different. It was as if he was proud of his situation—or as if he had crossed a line beyond which he could not be reached.

"You must have some mates, why don't you tell us about them?" Norri suggested.

"Nah, don't feel like it. You tell me about your wife, say. Or else give us a ciggie."

Leo rocked his leg, pleased with himself. He looked quickly at Harjunpaa sitting by the wall, as if to make sure that he was irritated. Harjunpaa stared out of the window, expressionless—Norri's windows faced north, you could see the TV complex and the link masts and the two water towers. In the distance, where the shimmering, bluish treeline began, was a high aerial with a rapidly blinking white light on the top. Harjunpaa fixed his eyes on that. He knew that Norri wasn't working in earnest yet, all he was doing was testing the boy, trying to draw anything useful out of him. Still he was sorry for Norri; the interview had continued like this for nearly an hour and a half. Mostly Leo had replied with one-liners like: "Get stuffed," "Fuck off," "Why don't you find out if you're interested."

There were moments when he almost hated Leo, like when he cocked his head and smirked, his smile an impenetrable mixture of satisfaction and scorn; he was quite sure that Leo had smiled the same way both in Kaisaniemi and at the pond. But that feeling passed quickly. He knew what was coming; they had the silver razorblade pendant, they had the footprint, some fingerprints, they had the pair of blood-stained jeans found in the cave, they had Leo's clothes, currently being examined in the lab, they had what the two little boys had told—he knew that there would come a moment when Leo's world would be even more desolate than ever before, when he'd

174

have nothing else but concrete walls and a dim, reinforced window, high up in the wall, nothing but his own
restless hands, tears.

"Maybe you should think about all this, so you understand what's involved."

"Go shoot yourself."

Somebody was talking outside in the corridor. Monica
said something and the voices were lowered. Steps approached the door and the buzzer went, although the
yellow light had been on. Norri sighed—maybe with relief—and walked to the door. Harjunpaa had time to see
Halme from section three and Monica—she looked serious, her eyes frightened, or shocked. Norri closed the
door when Halme started to explain. Harjunpaa went to
the window, beginning to get restless. He was certain that
Leo was one of the boys they had been after—but the
other one was still on the loose; he suspected Norri would
soon open the door, motion him out of the room, and say
in a low voice: "We'd better get going." He glanced at Leo
who for the first time seemed serious and was stealing
restless looks at the door.

Monica came in. She sat down where Harjunpaa had
been sitting and moved her head, pointing toward the
corridor—her eyes were wide and she looked at Harjunpaa as if to convey a message, only he did not understand
what it was. He stepped out. Norri, Halme, and Kangas
had moved a few steps away from the door.

Norri was clearing his throat. He was holding some
photographs, barely dry, and a sheet of lined paper,
folded once. Halme had a plastic bag that contained a
heavy, long-barreled revolver; in his other hand he
waved an envelope, by the sound of it there were coins
inside. They were all looking at Harjunpaa. Norri pushed
the paper at him. Harjunpaa unfolded and read. A tic
started in his eye.

175

Nothing in my life is worth all this agony. All I seem to do is hurt others. Me and Leo Melin killed that man near the pond, it just happened. We were going to beat up my father because he is such a shit but he didn't turn up.

What makes me glad is that all the time when we were giving it to him I thought it was Sod. Now he needn't come to my grave either since I'm a killer. We also beat up another man last week in Kaisaniemi because he wouldn't give us a bottle-opener. I don't know what happened to him. We left him lying there. I'm sorry I did these things, my heart is very heavy. Please give all my clothes and things to that dead man's kids, he said he had kids. And tell Ulla Lindberg who lives in Number 4 Kontukuja that I'll always love her and no hard feelings. And don't feel sorry for me. Now you can go abroad for your holidays even in wintertime because you don't have to worry about me getting up to something, or about who will cook food for me. I feel sorry for mother. I leave these two marks for Sod, it's payment for the bullet so he needn't grieve over it.

Miku

Harjunpaa took the photographs. He swayed as if he had been hit. The first was a close-up of the dead boy's face; he recognized it at once, didn't want to see any more. His hands fell down.

"I know him," he said in a dull voice. "He was in a stolen car. We had him. He's Mikael Bergman, a policeman's son. How could I have known?"

"Monica told us."

Harjunpaa pushed the photographs into the hands that were closest. Then he turned away and walked slowly to the nearest empty room, and rested his head against the windowpane. The glass was cool. Outside a man was drilling through the rock. In the corridor he heard Halme explaining, "I rang the father at work and all he said was, 'I see, well, I better get there to clear up the mess.' And he said that to him the boy had ceased to exist the night he picked him up from here. It really was a break-in to that gun room, even the cupboard had been forced—in that sense you can't blame him. Mrs. Bergman

176

had been at the hairdresser's, she's in shock now. All I could get out of them is that the boy had disappeared the night he was caught in the stolen car, and that the father had refused to report it. That the father had taken a bucket of water to the balcony, sloshed it down, and said, 'That's that done with.' It seemed to me his biggest worry was to get his gun back as soon as possible."

The man outside had finished drilling. In the face of that huge rock his task seemed hopeless. But if you looked to the left you could see that the man and his mate had already achieved something, that the rough lines of a foundation were already there, in the granite.

25

"You mean, killed himself?" asked Thurman. He looked suspicious, maybe secretly pleased too, or relieved or triumphant. "Well, he might just as well have done it a couple of weeks earlier."

Monica stared out through the windscreen and said nothing. Harjunpaa shifted on the back seat, staring at his hands. He remembered that Mikael's hands had been small and soft, like a child's, and yet they had held a bottle, a stone, the butt of that heavy revolver—they had been hands too small to be left so alone. Mikael had called Ulla Lindberg "Mummy." Harjunpaa sighed unhappily; what if Pauliina or Valpuri would one day call some other man "daddy."

Thurman said in a somewhat defensive tone, "What I mean is that then those two geezers would still be alive."

They were on their way to the morgue. The traffic was beginning to swell in anticipation of the afternoon rush hour. After a lengthy silence Thurman asked, "Are we going there for his fingerprints?"

"Yes," Harjunpaa spoke quietly. "And clothes. And shoes. The police surgeon said he'll have a preliminary look to see if there are any marks that could have been made in connection with these two incidents—maybe the victims had time to hit back or something."

Harjunpaa's voice faded. He remembered what Ulla Lindberg had said about Mikael's legs. The car radio tingled the two-tone warning of a general message. Monica turned the volume up.

"Central needs a free car in South Haaga. A man has been shot in Artturi Kanniston Street, Number 8. Any free cars in that part of town?"

"Shit," Thurman grunted, glancing at Monica and Harjunpaa. "We're almost there, barely a mile out."

Harjunpaa had no time to respond before Thurman was fingering the dashboard and the blue flash was on; Monica was holding the microphone. Before the siren blasted Harjunpaa had time to hear her say: "Central 8-9-1, SUOPO and technical, we are in the vicinity and heading toward the shooting incident. Have you any more information?"

Then the siren was in full flow, its noise battering Harjunpaa's ears. He could hear only bits of Central's reply: ". . . reported by a worried neighbor, but . . . on the floor, head in a pool of blood . . . ambulance with a doc is on its way . . . remember when you go in . . . some help for you on its way. . . ."

Thurman squeezed the car with skill through a set of red traffic lights at a big junction. It seemed to Harjunpaa that somewhere far down in Mannerheimintie another flashing blue light was approaching. Then they passed the fire station and sped along the narrow streets of Haaga, the wailing of the siren preceding them. Harjunpaa sat with a set face; he had a pain in his stomach. He also had an uncertain feeling that he was being punished for something.

Thurman thumbed the siren off.

"There."

He stepped on the brakes and swung the car alongside the pavement. They had arrived at a low apartment building with a space at the front, planted with trees. Some twenty people had gathered outside the B-staircase;

179

an old man was holding the door wide open. Automatically Harjunpaa registered the fact that the crowd was excited but that there was no panic. He began to be sure that this wasn't necessarily a crime—maybe a suicide, maybe an accident. Thurman was already out of the car, hand on hip, asking in a loud voice: "Does anybody know what's happened?"

Harjunpaa moved quickly toward the door, scanning the windows as he ran, not seeing anything alarming. Monica was close behind.

"On the third floor. Shot himself."

People followed them in. The staircase echoed with shuffling feet, hushed voices bounced back from the walls. On the first landing all doors were open and men, women, and children stood in the doorways. A dog was barking; in some flat a radio gave the time signal. The sound of an ambulance came from outside. On the second landing an old woman was standing by herself, pressing a hand on her heart. She motioned anxiously upward.

"Up there. He's on the floor, in the sitting room. They're all there."

"Was it you who called the police?"

"Yes. I heard the bang. I rang their doorbell. The little boy opened the door. I saw immediately . . ."

"You wait here."

On the third landing one of the three doors was wide open. There was a smell of cooking. Light streamed from the flat—all the windows faced the sun, which filled the place with sunshine. Dust danced in sunrays. On the floor in the hall there was a deflated children's beach ball, a wet towel, a rubber duck, and some sand. Underneath the clothes rack squatted a small boy, hugging his knees. Harjunpaa stopped and bent down while Monica and Thurman rushed in past him.

"You're not hurt anywhere, are you?"

180

The boy stared at Harjunpaa with wide eyes, didn't cry, didn't speak. He was perhaps five or six, maybe a little older, old enough to need to tag along with father, to be shown how to knock a nail off a plank and how bees build their nests. Harjunpaa touched the boy's hand. Sun and sand had made the skin rough. He took a deep breath, closing his eyes; he knew what this boy might become in a few years' time—tall and skinny, avoiding people's eyes, his heart full of craving and hunger for something he didn't have. And if all went as it so very easily did, he might end up on a plastic chair, dressed in overalls, seeing only eyes that did not want to find anything good in him.

"Wait here," Harjunpaa said in a low voice. "Don't go away. I'll be back and we'll think of something together."

The wailing sirens stopped. Harjunpaa went in.

The man lay on the floor next to the sofa. He was lying on his stomach and his head was turned away. He wore only a pair of soiled jeans; the upper part of his body was bare and so were his feet. Underneath the head there was a puddle of blood, next to his hand a small-caliber gun. Something was trying to work its way into Harjunpaa's consciousness, struggled hard but didn't quite make it, remained an irritation at the back of his mind. Thurman stood up from where he had knelt, next to the body. He wiped his fingers with a piece of tissue.

"No need for a doctor here. It's gone in through the top of the mouth, the bullet is still in the head."

Two girls sat by the kitchen table, the smaller one whimpering with fright. A woman stood next to the cooker, Monica by her side, asking something. The woman was preparing a salad; her movements were mechanical and she sounded as though she were in a trance when she started to speak. Thurman was popping flashbulbs. Ambulance men rushed in—suddenly the place was overrun by men in white coats, carrying black cases;

brisk movement and whispered words. Harjunpaa was leaning against the doorway and breathing with difficulty. He thought that the same group had visited another scene of a suicide some hours earlier, in the home of a boy called Mikael Bergman, and soon after it would go to yet another place, and sooner or later the man lying on the floor, the man for whom they had come, would be called Leo.

Harjunpaa turned back to the kitchen. The woman had shifted her position, favoring one foot; she was still tearing the lettuce for a salad—the green pieces fell to the floor, one after another.

". . . had his gun many a time," she whispered to Monica, automatically, as if she wasn't quite aware it was she who was talking. "But it became a real problem about a fortnight ago. He'd been drinking then, too, got back home one morning in a dreadful state . . . he claimed he'd been forced into an ambulance and had been injected . . . all day long he would sit and brood and examine himself—that vaccine was eating his insides, so he said. I said he should go into care but not him . . . instead he went to all the authorities, to the medical board, and fire brigade, and police; sure enough he was laughed out of every place, nobody would listen to him . . . that's when it started, his depression. . . ."

Harjunpaa took hold of the wall with one hand and pressed the other against his heart. There was a humming in his ears, as if giant sea shells were being held against them.

26

Harjunpaa pushed his bicycle up the road.

He had left it at the railway station in the morning and someone had pinched the air valve—he had noticed it as soon as he stepped down from the train. For a long while he had stood by his bike, undecided. He hadn't felt anything much—neither anger nor hostility; he guessed that the valve had been pinched by someone like Mikael or Leo, someone who didn't get much out of life, who in the end was just what he had been made into.

He pushed his bike and the back tire flapped against the road. The sound it made was like a mocking song, stinging him at every step.

It was very late, nearly dark; only a narrow band of light still remained in the west after the sunset. Harjunpaa reached the top of the hill. It had been raining earlier that evening; the road was still wet and the air smelled of green plants and soil. Ahead, in the bottom of the valley a small brook ran, mist shimmering above it. He didn't have far to go now, the rows of terraced houses could already be seen on his right; the houses were some way from the heart of the village, between a field and the woods and the cliffs.

He took a shortcut between the houses, along strange footpaths, until he reached his own familiar garden path. All the houses had two stories; they were painted red and at this time of night they seemed peaceful and reassuring.

His house was last in the row; behind it was the hill and the dark forest; all the windows were dark.

But Elisa was outside. She was sitting on the steps, still, arms wrapped around her knees—almost invisible in the dusk. You could tell she had been waiting for a long time. Harjunpaa wondered if anything had happened, but he couldn't—or didn't have the energy to—wonder what. He left his bike leaning against the shed wall and stood there, stupidly, without a word. Elisa seemed at peace, yet there was something, something odd or knowing or excited about her.

"Timo."

Harjunpaa stepped closer and bent down in front of her, spent. He rested his hands in Elisa's lap. She held his wrists with her dry cool hands.

"We're going to have a baby."

Harjunpaa stared ahead with unseeing eyes. Then he slipped down to his knees and laid his head on her lap; he felt he was sinking, his throat was dry and his eyes were stinging. His mind was crowded with all the children of that day: Mikael who was no longer, the little boy sitting under the clothes rack, the little girls round the table, Leo who was now in a concrete cell behind locked steel doors. Each one had once started as something a wife had told her husband about, each one had been carried for nine months, expected, each one was surrounded by good wishes at birth. Elisa took her hands from her lap and put them on his neck, rubbing gently.

"Timo?"

She had noticed that the backs of her hands were wet.

"They can take the coil out, it's no danger to the baby."

Harjunpaa still didn't speak; instead he buried his head deeper. Elisa's hand stopped. In a little while she said uncertainly: "You do want it, you don't think we should—"

"No," he said hoarsely. He had been so very unhappy,

as if something had been irrevocably lost—but now there was something growing amidst the desolation, something that warmed his heart.

He thought how the child was there, so near, only a few inches away—or not yet a child, just an embryo, but soon it would have all the features of a small human being, nose and eyes, fingers and toes, everything—all that would emerge and grow even though he and Elisa and her doctor had done their best to avoid its conception and growth, to prevent all those actions it would one day undertake, to negate all the things this child would now do and which they couldn't even begin to guess. They had been wrong, had presumed more than they knew. And yet Harjunpaa felt they had been reprieved.